to find a
MOUNTAIN

DATE DUE			

to find a
MOUNTAIN

DANI AMORE

LAKE UNION
PUBLISHING

Text copyright © 2014 Dani Amore
All rights reserved.

Published by Lake Union Publishing, Seattle

www.apub.com

Amazon, the Amazon logo, and Lake Union Publishing are trademarks of Amazon.com, Inc., or its affiliates.

ISBN-13: 9781477825761
ISBN-10: 1477825762

Cover design by Mumtaz Mustafa

Library of Congress Control Number: 2014939986

Printed in the United States of America

*This book is dedicated to two of the bravest people
I have ever known: my mother and my father*

PROLOGUE

—

My name is Benedetta. In Italian, in the dialect spoken around Casalvieri, where I'm from, it means "blessed." Can I say my God-given name was a wise choice, that my mother and father accurately predicted the life that I would lead? Yes and no, for I have known great joy as well as great tragedy.

I know that I have six beautiful children. Children who grew up in a household full of love, where there was always plenty of food, good food, on the table, and plenty of laughter. Some pain, too, but that is unavoidable. Your life cannot be full without pain.

I know that I have lived a long life. I consider that a very blessed thing, for I have known too many people, people I have loved, who did not make it nearly as far.

Today I laid my husband of fifty-one years to rest. He took good care of me and our children. I will miss him. The priest talked about the duty of the living to carry on the memory of the dead. I do that every day. I have done that every day of my life.

It is late now. The sun is dropping behind the Estero River, sinking like a giant orange stone. The warm breeze is making small ripples in the water. A boat putts up the river, its driver looking at the houses that line the river's banks. He occasionally turns his head forward to see where he's going. He should be more careful. There are many stumps in this stretch of the river, stumps that can rip a hole in the hull of a small boat. It's a sound the big river alligators look forward to.

The driver of the boat looks at my house as he passes but registers no expression. He probably sees the pool on the lower level of the screened-in porch, and most likely does not see the old woman sitting on the upper balcony, a small cup of espresso next to her, as she scribbles in the small, leather-bound journal.

My children are asleep, and so are their children. We are all tired from the exhaustion of the funeral, the crying, the chasing after the younger children who did not realize the meaning of the occasion that has brought us all together for the first time in many years. As I watched my children try to explain to my grandchildren the concept of death, it hurt me. We should all try to put off learning what death is for as long as possible.

A significant part of me died with my husband. I believe that whenever someone you love dies, a part of you goes with them. I also think that every time someone new is brought into your life, a part of you is reborn. The circle of life and death is a balancing act, God's way of making things even.

I have six children and eleven grandchildren now. From the looks in the eyes of my children and their spouses at the funeral, I'm sure there will be more on the way. There is something about a funeral that makes people remember the fragile nature of life, and in turn makes them want to create life again.

It was that way after the war in Italy. Entire towns laid to waste. Families destroyed. Dreams shredded by bullets and shrapnel. My children know very little of what happened to me during that time. The parts I have told them are the truth, but I have not told them everything.

They know that their father and mother met during the war. I was just a girl then, a young teenager, and their father was only a little older. My children know that their parents fell in love during that time, and although they think they know all the details, they don't. They will learn here, for the first time, all of the incredible, painful, unforgettable truths that I now feel it is time for them to learn.

They do not know how close to death I came. They do not know how close to death their father came. They do not know how close to death my entire village came—all because of the events that took place in my house the year the Germans arrived.

My children will learn that wars are fought not just on the front lines, but also in the dirt streets of poverty-stricken towns like Casalvieri, Italy.

They will learn that their mother killed a man during the war.

That is the purpose of this journal. I first want to get everything on paper, bring it out from the dusty parts of my brain. Once it is organized, I will let them read it for themselves.

I loved my husband with all my heart, and there is an emptiness now inside me that will forever prevent me from being whole again. And that is the way it should be. I look around my house and I see him. His eyes. His smile. His voice. I can hear him calling my name.

When my children scatter tomorrow, the silence in the house will be difficult, no matter how busy I make myself.

It is late. The memories are already coming back to me. The sounds of machine guns, airplanes, and bombs dropping from the sky. Remembering it all makes me feel both old and young, the way I felt so many years ago, when the Second World War came home to us in Casalvieri.

PART ONE

CHAPTER ONE

—

Casalvieri, Italy, 1943

The Germans arrived one fall morning and took control of Casalvieri without a single shot fired.

I woke up to voices coming from downstairs. I was close enough to understand parts of the conversation, but some of the words were spoken with a thick foreign accent that I had never heard before. It was not a strange thing for me then; my father was the unofficial leader of the village, a village too small really to have any kind of government, and he frequently had visitors coming to him, some at all hours of the morning or night.

There were two rooms upstairs; one was for my father, the other for me; my sister, Iole; and my brother, Emidio. Looking over at their bed, I could see they were still asleep, huddled together for warmth.

I kicked off the sheets and put on a heavy sweater, then my shoes. Halfway down the stairs, I could glimpse the big table in the kitchen where our family ate all of our meals. It was a sturdy table with dents and scrapes that lightened the dark, rich wood and marked the many years of use it had seen. My father had been born on that very table, and we had literally grown up around it.

My first image of the visitors was the shoulder of a gray uniform and a matching gray hat with a black visor. Not knowing much about armies and uniforms, I nonetheless knew enough to recognize the clothes as belonging to a soldier. And then I heard another language that was guttural, with occasional sharp-sounding words.

And I knew.

There had been much talk recently of the Germans establishing a line of defense across the middle of Italy. Casalvieri was several miles north of Mt. Cassino, the highest point in central Italy, with a commanding view over the Mignano Gap, the most direct route north to Rome. Whoever owned Mt. Cassino owned the Mignano Gap. And whoever owned the Mignano Gap owned the right of passage from southern Italy to Rome. And whoever owned Rome owned Italy.

This is what the men talking with my father had said. I hadn't completely understood it all, but I felt like I knew the basics.

The talk had centered on the threat of an Allied capture of Sicily and other islands in the Mediterranean, and how they would work their way up to us.

If it was true, the Germans would be taking over small towns like Casalvieri along a line cutting east to west across Italy.

Judging from the presence of German officers in our kitchen, I assumed the talk was true.

As I continued down to the bottom of the stairs, my father's voice boomed out. "Benny! Come, come meet our guests!"

I walked into the kitchen and eating area, one long room that functioned as our primary living space. At one end of the rectangular room stood the table, and at the other end was the fireplace, over which we cooked all of our meals. On an iron rack next to the fireplace hung the pots, pans, and cooking utensils.

My father was standing next to the kitchen table with two men. One was a big man with a full belly, silver hair, and a ruddy complexion. He was tall, well over six feet, and I could see small veins in his cheeks, usually the sign of too much drinking. The other man was thin and pale with fair hair that matched the colorless gray of his eyes. He was tall, but not as tall as the first. Next to them, my father looked even shorter and rounder than he normally did.

"This is my daughter Benedetta," my father said. "Benedetta, this is Colonel Wolff." I shook hands with the large, ruddy man. "And this is Lieutenant Becher," my father said, and I shook hands with the thin German soldier.

"A beautiful daughter," Wolff said, as the men took their seats at the table. "How many children do you have, Signor Carlesimo?" He had a heavy accent, but his Italian was surprisingly good. His voice was gravelly, and he sounded tired, but there was a pleasant smile on his face.

"Three," Papa said.

"And your wife . . . ?"

"She died with the fourth."

I had retrieved the coffeepot from the small wire hook that held it over the fire. The metal was chipped and dented, scratched here and there, but it still worked. Like my father, it had survived, and showed its years, but kept its history to itself. He rarely spoke of Mama, and I knew that he wished not to speak of her now.

"Here's your coffee, Papa."

I refilled his cup and offered to do the same for the Germans, but they waved me away. I turned my back on them and felt their eyes follow me.

"It will be nice to have such beauty with coffee in the morning, Signor Carlesimo," the thin one, Becher, said. His Italian came out stilted and awkward, but his message was easily understood.

I turned and watched my father struggle to maintain an impassive expression. My head swam.

The Germans would be living with us.

In our house.

My stomach churned as I worked out the logic of it. Our house was on the highest hill overlooking the valley of Cassino below. From here, the Germans could watch anyone coming or going. Plus, there were more rooms on the other side of the house that were spacious but drafty; we had basically sealed them off and turned them into storage areas. My father had spoken of emptying them out and turning them into living quarters, but it was too big a job for us. The Germans certainly had enough hands to get the job done.

I already feared for my father's safety. The Germans were known to force Italian civilians into the hardest, most dangerous labor on the front. Carrying ammunition and gasoline, retrieving the wounded. They saw the Italians as a good way to conserve their own forces. Better an Italian man died on the front than a German.

Trying to sound casual, but certainly not succeeding, I managed to utter one short sentence. "And you will be staying until . . . ?" There was an awkward silence as I gestured, but no other sound came from my mouth.

Wolff looked at me curiously, smiling slightly, but it was Becher who answered, with ice in his voice.

"Until we have won the war, of course."

CHAPTER TWO

—

When I was excused, I flew up the stairs two at a time and rushed into our room, where Iole and Emidio were rolling on the bed, wrestling and giggling. The look on my face must have terrified them, because Emidio's lower lip started to tremble, like it always did just before he burst into tears.

"Iole," I said to my sister. "Put Mama's crucifix behind the dresser, and get her jewelry box—put it under the loose floorboard in the closet. You know the one?"

She nodded but stood still. They both looked at me, eyes wide, and then a big tear slowly slid down Emidio's cheek.

I forced myself to relax, then went and got Mama's jewelry box myself, lifted up the floorboard in the closet, and slid the box inside.

"I'm sorry about that, you two."

Just then, I heard footsteps coming up the stairs. I hugged my brother and sister to my chest and listened.

Papa stepped into the room and closed the door behind him.

I fought it desperately, but my lower lip was determined to tremble like Emidio's. And when Iole saw me, hers started, too.

"Shush, you three," my father said. He knelt in front of us and his expression was calm, his big brown eyes warm and smiling. My heart burst with love at the sight of his gentle face, reassuring us as always.

"Listen, the Germans are not here to hurt us," he said. "They have chosen our house because of its position on the hill."

"Chosen our house . . . for what?" Emilio said.

"They will be living here with us," I said.

"In our house?" Iole asked.

"Yes. It will be fine," our father said. "It is no surprise. Here, they can watch people coming through the valley. Most of the soldiers will be on Mt. Cassino. They will only use Casalvieri as a place to bring the wounded. They will probably set up a makeshift hospital at the Ingrelli house. Colonel Wolff, Lieutenant Becher, and a few men will stay with us. They're going to be staying in the rooms downstairs."

"For how long?" Iole asked.

"Until they win the war," I answered.

From outside, we heard the sound of a vehicle starting up.

Papa went to the window and looked out, then came back and knelt in front of us again. "They say that if we help them, they will help us. And I believe them. They have food and, more importantly, good medical supplies."

I immediately thought of Mama, and I could tell that Papa did, too.

"We just have to be careful." He fixed his eyes on my younger brother and sister. "Iole. Emidio. I want this room spotless before you come downstairs," he said. "Benedetta, come with me."

We went next door to his room. It smelled of Papa: a mixture of wine, garlic, and a man who works hard every day. Every once in a while, though, when a soft breeze made its way through the house, usually in the springtime, I could smell my mother. I often came into Papa's room on those kinds of days, just to see if I could detect her scent.

I sat on his bed and Papa pulled an old wooden chair over and sat in front of me.

"Benedetta, you have to be strong." He took my hands in his. "They are scared of us. The people who live here, all Italians. They don't know who are *ribelli* and who aren't." The *ribelli* were the rebels, young Italian men and a few women who opposed Mussolini and vowed to do everything they could to kill Germans.

His eyes clouded over. "But it is not a good thing that they fear us. With fear comes danger. You know how a wild animal attacks viciously when backed into a corner? That's what these *Germanesi* will do—if we fight them. Colonel Wolff said that if one of his men dies, ten of us will die."

I flinched at the idea of the Germans killing ten of us, but my father's grip on my hands tightened.

"If we feed them, wash their clothes, their bedding, help them find their way around, they will treat us right," he said.

"But Papa," I said. "Will they make you go to the front line? That's what I heard they do."

His smile was different this time, not relaxed like always, and because of that, I knew he was afraid.

"Benny," he said, "listen to me. I am not going to the front line. The Germans need me to help them with the people here. They consider me the leader of the village, and as soon as I'm done talking with you, I need to go around and start collecting food for them until their supplies arrive."

"What happens then?" I asked.

"What do you mean?"

"What happens when they are organized, the village is giving them what they want—they won't need you anymore. What then?"

Now he made no attempt to smile.

"Once they are here and are organized, it is true they may not need me as much. When that time comes"—he shrugged—"we shall see. I may have to find a mountain."

Fear struck at my stomach like I'd been kicked by a mule.

"Papa, if you go, who will take care of us?" I asked, gesturing at the next room, where Iole and Emidio were probably already wrestling once more.

Papa rose to his feet and looked down at me. His brown eyes revealed nothing.

He answered matter-of-factly.

"You."

CHAPTER THREE

——

In a small village like Casalvieri, word traveled fast. It seemed like my father had been gone no more than five minutes when people started bringing bundles of food to the house. And, of course, along with their bundles of sausages, bread, eggs, cheese, and wine, they brought plenty of questions.

"Will they kill us?"

"What are they like?"

"Why did they pick your house?"

"Will we have to go to the front?"

"Will they burn down our houses and rape the women when they leave?"

It was almost too much to bear. I answered the questions I could answer, and to the ones I couldn't I said, "Why don't you just ask the *Germanesí* yourself?"

I usually got a blank stare, followed by a peek around my shoulder.

For the next hour, people continued to bring baskets of food to the house, and I struggled to organize them. The big table was piled high with bundles by the time visitors stopped coming.

At long last, Alberta Checcone stopped in. She was a short woman, my father's age, with a round face and varicose veins in her legs. She was thick, but not fat, and at one point in her life had probably been somewhat pretty. But time had not been kind to Signora Checcone. She had lost her husband to tuberculosis, an illness that had taken many years to blossom before killing him suddenly, leaving his wife no children, a small house, and a small patch of land.

She took care of herself: She planted the crops, harvested, made her own wine, and did the hundreds of things a woman by herself needs to do. She was loved by everyone in town, and perhaps pitied by a few. I adored her, as did Iole and Emidio. Since my mother's death, she came to the house more often, helping my father and us. And when she needed a man to help her, usually my father was the one.

We had gotten to know and like her so much that we called her "Zizi" Checcone, a more familiar form of "Zia," which meant aunt.

Now, she placed her own small bundle on the table.

"Come walk with me, Benedetta," she said. "I have another bundle at home I need your help with."

We walked out in the midmorning sun and I slowed my pace to walk beside her.

"How are they treating you?" she asked, as soon as we were out of earshot of the house.

"They have hardly spoken a word to me. This Colonel Wolff told me to bake bread. Other than that, they have left me alone."

We quickly reached her house and went inside. She turned to me and held my hands tightly.

"Listen to me, Benny, you must be careful. You must be strong. You must be brave. But above all, you must be careful."

"But Papa is here . . ."

"For now. But he must leave soon. Like the other men," she said.

"What do you mean?"

"Have you not noticed?" she asked.

I shook my head.

"The fields? They are empty."

Suddenly, I realized how silent the village had been this morning. Without really thinking, I had perhaps assumed the Germans had forced people to stay in their homes, or maybe that the people of my small village were hiding, but the opposite was true.

"The men . . ." I began.

Zizi Checcone sighed, a heavy, tired sigh.

"The men have gone to the mountains."

The men. No one was going to work in the fields.

"But how will we survive?" I asked.

My mind was whirling. If the men weren't working in the fields, there would be no crops. With no crops, there would be no food. With no food, we would starve.

"We will survive, Benedetta. But we must be crafty. Here." She walked back to the stairway leading from the dining room to the upstairs. She pulled back a board and I saw a cubbyhole filled with a bag of flour, salted pork, and jars of tomatoes.

"You must find something like this in your house. If you are in charge of the Germans' food, steal just enough to survive. But be very, very careful."

Suddenly I felt nauseated and could feel the tears running down my face. I didn't want to be left alone without my father. I had already lost my mother. I needed help. I needed someone to take care of me.

"Benny." Zizi Checcone took me into her arms and patted my back. The cloth of her dress smelled clean. "Benny. I'm sorry if I scared you. But you need to be prepared. We need to be prepared."

She released me and gathered up the bundle of extra food for me to take back home, back to the strange men living in my house.

"I am here for you. Even if your father does go with the men to the mountain, do not feel that you are alone. In fact, I will see if I can come and live with you. If the *Germanesi* allow it."

I thanked her and walked slowly back to my house, my feet like slabs of stone. The sun felt even warmer and there was a hint of dust in the air. Despite what Zizi Checcone said, I felt alone. Completely and wholly alone.

CHAPTER FOUR

—

I used to have a lot of friends. After my mother died I began to see less and less of them. Most girls my age were just starting to take over some of the responsibilities their mothers traditionally bore. I had taken over all of them.

There was no point in complaining about it. What would Papa have said or been able to do about it? In my family, work was not something to be avoided.

Of all my friends, Lauretta Fandella was the only one who had truly remained so. She was a tall, big-boned girl with a long face and thick features. Pretty, but in a rough way. Her shoulders were broad and her feet were long and wide; it was the kind of body that generations of ancestors working in these fields and mountains had developed, then passed down to their descendants. Lauretta Fandella was already a typical farm woman and she was only sixteen years old. If there had ever been a girl born to work the fields and raise five or six children, working day and night, drinking wine and living life without a care in the world other than pure survival, it was Lauretta.

The door to the Fandella house was open and I knocked, heard a voice call out, then I went inside.

Lauretta had three older brothers, all of them tall and lanky like her; they were rumored to be *lazzaroni*, kept in check only by their father, who was bigger and tougher than all of his sons. At least for now. But when I went inside the house, only Lauretta's mama was there, sitting at the table sewing a sweater. She nodded her head upstairs and I climbed the rickety staircase, then went down the short hallway to Lauretta's room. The door was closed and I knocked. She opened the door immediately, able to reach across the small room from her bed and grasp the doorknob without getting up.

Her room, not much bigger than a closet, was taken up mostly by her bed and, in the corner, a small table upon which sat her clothes. The only other objects were a crucifix over her bed and, on the opposite wall, a poster of the singer Enrico Caruso.

There was no doubt in my mind that Lauretta was obsessed with boys. She talked about them, thought about them, even, according to her, dreamed about them.

Lauretta was sitting on the edge of the bed, a mirror propped on the small table in front of her. She was doing her hair, braiding it back in a long ponytail. Lauretta's beautiful long black hair was probably her best feature.

"Let me guess," I said. "You heard about the *Germanesi*?"

She smiled and rolled her eyes at me, continuing to work on her hair. I noticed she had on a short dress that looked like it had been recently pressed.

"What, are you getting ready for an inspection?" I asked.

"I just figured the Germans would want to see some of the sights, if you know what I mean."

"You're terrible."

"It's a duty—we need to represent our country properly," she said, pushing her breasts up higher in her bra.

"Lauretta, these aren't the local boys. These are men who have seen much fighting and death. You should be careful how you act around them."

"What are they like, the officers who are staying at your house?"

"Two officers, a couple soldiers. The officers seem pleasant enough. One is a big, older man, very nice. The other is thin and wiry. He looks kind of mean. I wouldn't want to be his enemy."

"Do you think they will treat you—"

"As long as we do what they want, they will tolerate us," I said. "Nothing less, nothing more."

"Be thankful, Benedetta," she said. "They already took over the Ingrelli house and are turning it into a hospital. The family had to move in with the Carbonis. At least you are still in your own house."

"I don't feel it is our house any longer."

I sat down on the bed next to her and helped her put the finishing touch on her braid.

"My father has left," she said. "He told us it was time for him to find a mountain."

"I heard that many of the men are doing that."

"It's that or die holding a German gun."

"The Germans think we are dogs," I said.

"Then my father is a dog who bites the hand that feeds him," she said.

"What do you mean?"

"I mean he hates the Germans," Lauretta said. "His brother was killed by some of Mussolini's *fascisti*. Ever since then, he has hated Mussolini and his black shirts, and when Il Duce joined up with Hitler—well, now my father hates Germans."

"Don't say that so loud," I said. "They told my father that for every German soldier who dies, ten of us will be executed."

Lauretta looked at me as if I were ten years younger than her, not two.

21

"Well, Benedetta, I don't think Papa is foolish enough to kill any of *these* Germans."

"I'm not sure that matters."

"Just make sure you don't repeat anything I've said—Papa would not be pleased with me, or with you," she said.

Lauretta stood up, smoothed her dress, then turned and twisted several times in front of the mirror. She put her arm around me and pulled me over so that we were both reflected in it. I looked small and worried compared to Lauretta.

"What do you think?" she asked.

"Unfortunately, I think the Germans will be more than happy to try to take in some of the local color."

CHAPTER FIVE

——

I left Lauretta's house and walked along the outer edge of Casalvieri, the part of the village that hugged the side of the mountain. I walked past houses where people waved to me, wearing apprehensive expressions that told me they were carrying on because that's all they knew how to do.

I looked down to the valley below, normally a peaceful, sleepy view. Now clouds of dust wafted to and fro, and I could hear the sound of machinery, tanks, and jeeps as they went about their business, destroying everything in their path on the way to Mt. Cassino.

Men had been fighting over this land for thousands of years. These rocks, this dirt, all of it would still be here long after the blood from these men had been covered in dust. Only their bones would survive, and those too would be buried for eternity in the dank tomb of the soil, while the trees and the rocks would feel the warmth of the sun thousands of years from now.

A breeze blew around me, taking the edge from the sun's hot rays off my shoulders.

My foot kicked a small pebble and it rolled in front of me, going down a small hill before trickling off to the side of the path. I circled the village, saw my own house in the distance, then walked farther up the mountain, veering off the path to a small plateau, a shelf with a small grove of trees and flowers.

An iron gate marked the entrance to the cemetery.

Thick oak fencing, falling down in some places, encircled the rows of tombstones and crude markers. The first headstones to greet visitors were the oldest. They were uneven—some sat high, others were sunken as the ground continued to shift over the years. These stones marked the village's ancestors, some going back hundreds of years.

The farther you walked in, the more recent the dates on the headstones became.

My mother's grave was on the last row.

Next to her was an empty space, probably for my father. On the other side of her were the two Vito children, twins, who had died the year before of food poisoning. The entire village had turned out for their funeral, even the weak, old, and crippled.

Whenever I visited my mother, I wondered if she was taking care of the Vito twins in Heaven. Probably. If there were children who needed to be taken care of, I was sure she would be the one to step in and give them what they needed. One time, in an old book about animals, I saw an illustration of some kind of bird who was ripping chunks of flesh off her own body to feed her children. That was Mama.

On the walk over, I had picked a flower for her, and now I placed it next to her headstone. It was a modest marker, plain granite with simple block letters carved into the stone. Sofía Carlesimo. 1901–1941.

Mama was born in a small town about ten miles away called Agavita. Her family had been farmers, and at a festival put on by all of the churches of the area, she had met my father. My mother was a year away from being of proper age, so they courted and then married on her birthday.

She listened now, I was sure, as I told her all about the arrival of the *Germanesí*. Sometimes I said the words out loud; more often than not I sent the thoughts to her from my mind rather than through the air. She heard about my fear for Papa, my anxiety over what they would do to us if they ever left Casalvieri. Or if they stayed too long.

I traced the grass over her grave with my hand, imagining our hands connecting through the many feet of dirt and rock. I wanted her strength to rise up and flow through me.

Instead, a wave of anger, fear, and confusion washed over me. Like the sea in a rising storm, it grew in intensity. A cold sweat broke out along my brow, and the cemetery began to spin around me. I could feel my heart beating quickly; my breath was shallow. I clenched my fists, felt cold dampness on my palms, like wrung-out dishrags.

From my mouth came a sound, not a scream but a twisted, guttural moan that rose from the back of my throat.

Slowly, I felt the terror pass, and then my body sagged, fatigued and spent. The experience was not new to me; I'd been having these fits on and off since Mama passed away, but I told no one.

A twig snapped behind me and I twirled, expecting to see a German soldier coming at me. But nothing was there, just granite witnesses watching me impassively.

A bush rustled to my left and I looked but saw nothing. Then I heard, or thought I heard, the sound of boots on the dirt path receding farther away from me. The trees behind the last row of headstones swayed gently with a breeze and I looked at their leaves fluttering. In order to fit the next row of headstones, those trees would need to be cleared.

I wondered if, after all this was done—after the Germans were done with us—there would be enough room, even with all of the trees cleared, to fit the many new headstones that would need to go here.

And if mine would be among them.

CHAPTER SIX

—

When I got back home, the house was empty. Iole and Emidio were probably off with Papa, helping him talk to everyone in the village about what to do now that the Germans had taken over. I was sure Papa had his hands full dealing with the questions that were bound to be asked as the shock set in that the village was really no longer ours. On top of that, Papa had to deal with Emidio and Iole; Emidio had a knack for breaking things in other people's homes.

I went down into the cellar to get a jar of tomatoes to begin making lunch. One of the last things my mother had taught me was how to jar tomatoes. She did it a special way, separating the size of the tomato chunks. She would put the biggest ones in one jar, the medium-sized in a different jar, and the smallest ones, as well as the smashed pulp, into another. Then, depending on the importance of the occasion, she would retrieve the jar to match. The more special the occasion, the bigger the tomato chunks. I don't know if everyone in my village did it that way, but my mother was adamant that we should.

It was disappointing to see how low our food reserves were. We should have been stockpiling and hiding food in anticipation of the Germans' arrival, but the summer had been a dry one, and the one before that, too. Besides, no one had known with any certainty that the Germans would come. Up until now it had been speculation. But the hard truth was looking us all in the face and, with the men leaving for the mountains, the shelves were only going to get emptier.

I brought the tomatoes upstairs. I had chosen a jar that held the smallest chunks and pieces of pulp in honor of the *Germanesi*, knowing they wouldn't realize the significance. I put the jar on the counter next to the eggplant that I had cleaned yesterday, poured olive oil into a cast-iron skillet, then placed it over the small fire I had built in the oven. I chopped onion and garlic, then tossed them in. When they were browned, I poured the tomatoes and eggplant in also, stirring them until the flavors were well mixed. The sauce would be hearty and versatile, something I could use with pasta or as a base for stew.

Suddenly, I felt someone's presence in the room with me, and I turned, startled to see a man standing halfway between the big table and the kitchen. Somehow, he had made no sound entering the house.

He was a German soldier. He had blond hair and washed-out blue eyes that were rimmed with red. I guessed his uniform might have fit him when he joined the army, but now it looked a size too big for him. Judging by his face, he had seen some of the worst war has to offer.

His eyes were on my legs, and the look on his face scared me.

It reminded me of when we used to have an old dog named Fleek. One day, Fleek had managed to catch a bird in the backyard. I was outside doing laundry when he ran up to me, the bird struggling in his mouth, flapping its wings and kicking its feet in the air.

Old Fleek's usually gentle, tired eyes made contact with mine and there was a hungry, wild gleam in them that I had never seen before.

The soldier continued to look at me and I tugged on the bottom of my dress, trying to force it down farther over my thighs, but I knew it wasn't helping. I had grown so much in the last year that my legs had shot out from under the dress, but we didn't have the money to buy more material so I could make a new one. Stupid.

My breasts had grown considerably, too. My dress had been made for me when my chest was flat, breasts just slight bumps in the pleat. But now they strained against the flimsy fabric, the very top of each breast barely visible over the hemline.

I should have changed immediately when the Germans arrived, or at least thrown one of Papa's shirts over the top of my dress. Things were different now; I had to be more careful, I told myself. In this outfit, I was an advertisement for something I didn't want to be.

"Oh! I didn't hear you come in," I said, after a struggle to come up with something that would break the silence.

He didn't answer, but seemed to mumble something under his breath.

I moved to get the platter of bread that sat on the edge of the hearth to keep warm. The soldier followed me with his eyes, not responding. My heart was thudding in my chest. Next to the bread was a knife, designed to cut bread, not men, but it made me feel better to be close to it.

Instead of responding to me, the German looked behind him. My breath caught in my throat at the slow cunning of the movement. He was considering something that he didn't want the rest of the men, probably the two officers especially, to know about.

I picked up the bread knife and started cutting slices off the thick loaf. When he turned back to me, I'd put several on a plate and turned to him, the plate in one hand, the knife in the other, pointed directly at him.

His eyes were like rough hands on my breasts, then they moved down to my legs and thighs. He was fondling my entire body without actually touching me.

I could see his nostrils widening and narrowing as his breath came faster. There was sweat on his forehead.

For the first time since he'd entered the room, he looked at my face. He smiled, his lips revealing yellow, stained teeth. I felt like that bird that had been in Fleek's mouth, kicking and flapping but getting nowhere, no chance of escape.

I backed tighter against the counter and he came closer. He was almost within arm's length and I could see that his eyes were even more bloodshot than I had first noticed.

"Don't . . ." I started.

He laughed, a mean, hungry laugh. I got the feeling he was a man who would enjoy fighting a woman.

Then the house's main door scraped open, and the German froze. Heavy bootfalls crossed the threshold and then Colonel Wolff came through the entryway from the main room. He stopped when he saw us. His eyes went from the soldier to me, where they lingered, then softened, and I knew that he had recognized my fear.

The German reached past me and I involuntarily flinched. But his hand grasped the bread on the counter and he tore off a chunk, then held it up to Wolff by way of explanation.

Wolff looked at me, then back to the German. I eased away and stood as still as I could, but my knees were trembling.

Colonel Wolff said something to the soldier in German, and I heard the name Schlemmer. The soldier, Schlemmer, held up the bread again and pointed at me. Wolff responded angrily and I could tell he didn't believe whatever story Schlemmer was giving him.

With a final bark from Wolff, Schlemmer strode quickly from the room, never looking back at me.

Wolff walked over to the counter and got a piece of bread for himself, and poured a small cup of wine, then gestured for me to sit with him.

His Italian was broken and not my dialect, but I could understand him.

"My men are tired," he said. He shrugged. "But that is no excuse."

He sipped his wine and looked out the window.

I again tried to cover my thighs with the hem of my dress.

"They have seen too much death," he said. "They have been pushed too hard. And they are too young. Not as young as you, but still too young."

"He was going to hurt me," I said.

Wolff shook his head.

"No. Do not worry. My men will not touch you. I promise that to you, and I have promised that also to your father. We do not wish to harm anyone here, nor do we want anyone here to try to harm us."

"But they are a long way from home, a long way from their girlfriends . . ." I said, trying to explain and understand at the same time what had just happened.

"That's true, but that is not the reason for . . ." He waved vaguely at the part of the kitchen where Schlemmer had approached me.

"Schlemmer is a good boy," he said. "He was close with another boy. That boy had his head caved in by an American's shovel. Split the skull from the top all the way down to the neck."

I remembered the way Schlemmer had looked at me.

"He hasn't been the same since. He is scared. It just depends on what he chooses to do with that fear. It can make him grow stronger or it can destroy him."

Or it can destroy me, I thought.

"This bread is very good," he said.

I tried to smile, but my face felt tight.

He pushed his chair back and stood, stretching and grimacing as he did so. I picked up his empty cup and took it to the counter.

"Are you going to the front?" I didn't so much want to hear an answer. I was more scared of being alone again, despite what Wolff had promised to my father and me.

"Soon. Soon enough."

He made his way to the doorway and then looked back at me. I let my eyes fall to the floor, noting the rough-hewn wood, the flaws, the knots. So old, so much use.

"It gets drafty in here, no?" Wolff asked, gesturing around the kitchen.

"No, not . . ." I started, but then saw his look before he directed it elsewhere.

"Well, yes, yes, it can get breezy," I said, "what with the strong winds and the cracks in the rock."

He nodded at me. "Perhaps a shirt with sleeves . . ."

I nodded. "I think I will be much more comfortable in something like that."

He looked at me and a tired smile came to his face, and then he left.

CHAPTER SEVEN

—

My father walked through the door, and although the Germans had been with us less than four days, he suddenly looked ten years older. His shoulders, always slightly rounded, were now downright slumped. The bags under his eyes had turned dark, and the smile was gone from his face, along with the bounce in his step. My heart caught in my throat, but before I could ask what was wrong, he answered.

"Benedetta," he said. "I am going to the front."

"No . . ." I began, but he held up his hand.

"It is too late, Benny. I, we, have no choice."

"Why don't you find a mountain, Papa?" I whispered. "Like the other men. They are there; they can help you. You won't survive at the front!"

"The Germans have said if I were to disappear . . . well, it just would not be good."

"But why you? I thought they needed you to work with the people in Casalvieri . . ."

He shrugged. "They say they need me at the front, to coordinate the drivers of the ambulances."

"I need you! *We* need you . . ."

His eyes suddenly blazed with anger, but I was not scared; I knew it wasn't directed at me.

"And I need you, but these . . ." He lowered his voice to a whisper. "These machines don't think. They follow orders, and expect us to do the same."

We paused at the sound of boots scraping the gravel outside, but they, along with the voices of their two German owners, soon trailed off as the soldiers continued walking.

"Signora Checcone is going to come and stay with you," my father said. "With all of the cooking and cleaning for the Germans, you're going to need help. Plus, you need to take care of Iole and Emidio. Wolff has given me his word that you won't be harmed."

"Don't worry about me, Papa," I said, fighting back the urge to throw my arms around him and cry on his shirt.

"I will be back every few days or so, bringing the wounded back to the hospital at the Ingrellis'."

I wanted to ask if Wolff had said anything about the incident with Schlemmer. I considered it as my father talked to me, and I looked into his eyes. They were dark brown like mine, and they looked so rich, so wounded, so full of love and pain that my heart sagged as he talked. I wouldn't bring up what Schlemmer had done—especially since, technically, he hadn't done anything. Papa had enough to worry about, staying alive being at the top of the list.

"Iole and Emidio don't need to know where I'm going."

"What have you told them?"

"That I am going to neighboring villages to help the Germans."

But what if you don't come back? I thought, but again could not ask. He needed me to be strong. He was trying to be strong for all of us, as he had been since Mama died. Now it was time for someone else to be strong for him.

"Just remember, Papa," I said. "If the Germans put a gun in your hand, point the part where the bullet comes out *away* from you."

He smiled then, and laughed. I knew it was partly from relief, and partly from trying to make me feel calm and relaxed. It worked. But when I got up to start packing clothes for him, my legs were unsteady beneath me. Papa grabbed me and hugged me hard. The stale sweat in his collar seemed like the sweetest smell in the world to me at that moment. God couldn't take him away from me. He just couldn't.

Losing one of my parents was enough—too much, in fact.

I intended to keep this one.

CHAPTER EIGHT

—

I briefly forgot an Italian tradition, a way of life, and because of that I began to get angry with Zizi Checcone.

She arrived the day after my father left. I saw her trudging wearily up the hill toward the house with a bundle over her shoulder, and when I opened the door for her, her brow was beaded with perspiration and she was very short of breath. She had on a thick black dress, which had probably heated up quite well underneath the sun.

Emidio and Iole rushed past me to her and threw their arms around her thick waist and legs.

"Zizi Checcone, are you really going to stay with us?" Iole asked.

"If you want me to," she said, a small smile tugging at the corner of her mouth.

Both of them cried out, "Yes! Yes!"

She raised her black eyes toward me and I smiled at her.

"It's good to have you here, Zizi Checcone," I said. "Let me take your bag up to Papa's room."

"Oh, I don't need a room. I can sleep in the kitchen," she said. "Or maybe out here on the floor with a blanket . . ."

"Papa gave us strict instructions," I said. "You are to sleep in his room."

With that, I hoisted her bag over my shoulder and went up to Papa's room, which I had just cleaned.

When I came back down, Zizi Checcone was standing in front of the big table, her hands in front of her, looking at the big black pot being heated over the fire. I was about to start a batch of menestra, a soup that is cooked with whatever ingredients are available.

"How are you doing, Zizi Checcone?" I asked. I started chopping vegetables, making room for her beside me. But she didn't join me, as I'd expected her to. Instead, she took a seat at the table.

"I am well, Benedetta, thank you. There is always much work to be done, even though I am by myself and have no one else to take care of," she said. "The problem with that is there is also no one to help."

Talk about no help, I thought, hoisting another log onto the fire as she went on sitting in her chair, her hands folded in her lap.

She told me about how her land had not been properly prepared for crops and that was why her harvest had not been as bountiful as she hoped. For ten minutes she talked while I chopped garlic, sliced tomatoes, and cleaned vegetables, all with no offer of help from the woman who had been brought here specifically to help me.

"It is hard to be the head of a household," she said. "Much to do. Much responsibility. And it is not always easy to ask for help."

I nodded.

"When a man leaves, the woman is suddenly in charge, and she is not always ready for that."

I plunked beans into the soup that was still too thin. There was no point in listening to her; she was repeating herself.

"Women suddenly have to do things the world has not prepared them for," she said.

She was like a broken record, all this talk of women being heads of the household, that's what happens when men leave for the mountains. Suddenly, my hands froze.

Not easy to ask for help. I felt my face flush and turned to look at her. She had her eyes lowered; she was wringing her hands.

She was waiting for me to ask her to help. How foolish of me! Here I was getting angry with her, chastising her in my mind for being lazy and unhelpful, when she was simply being respectful toward me. Not wanting to overstep her bounds and insult me. Sometimes I was a stupid girl.

"Zizi Checcone," I said, and she looked up quickly. "Since my father is not here, I wonder if I could ask you to help me. There is so much to do for the Germans, for Iole and Emidio, for the house, I would appreciate any help you could give me."

She jumped up and her hand came out of a small bag next to her feet. In it was a jar of tomato sauce.

"I would love to," she said. "Let's start by thickening this soup up." She dumped the tomato sauce in.

"How much bread do we have?" she asked.

"I've got two loaves."

"Benedetta, why don't you start a fire in the bread oven and I will begin making the dough."

I started to go, but she stopped me.

"Is there much laundry to be done?" she asked.

"Piles and piles," I answered.

"Do you know how to clean clothes with ash from the fireplace?"

"What are you talking about?" I asked.

"When the bread is done, and after dinner, we will use the ash to clean the clothes," she said.

"How does that work?"

"We'll fill a large wooden tub with water outside, add the ash, bring it to a boil, and then the ash will sink to the bottom. When it does, the water above it will have a slick quality to it that cleans even the dirtiest clothes. Soap is very hard to come by these days."

"All right," I said. "I'll start the oven."

"Very good, Benedetta. Thank you."

I heard the tone of her voice and she was smiling at me, a twinkle in her eye.

"No, Zizi Checcone, thank you." I meant it. I knew I could learn a lot from Zizi Checcone.

I stepped outside, happy to have behaved properly (eventually) and displayed the manners my mother and father had taught me.

CHAPTER NINE

—

The big table was piled with meat.

The German soldiers fighting on the front line near Mt. Cassino were starving. Apparently the German army was already running low on fuel and the supply convoys to the front were all but halted. The Germans told us their men were in desperate need of meat and that they were weak from lack of proper food. They needed meat, and they needed it prepared in a way that would allow it to be packed for days, maybe even weeks and months, without spoiling.

Word went out into the village and soon women were arriving at the house with what little meat they had. Haunches of wild game. A few chickens. Tripe and sweetbreads. By the end of the day, the table in my house looked like something straight out of a slaughterhouse.

The butcher was on his way to show the Germans where to take the meat, and from there he would smoke and then cure it so that it could be taken to the front line. It was probably for this reason that the butcher had not been told to pick up a gun and join the Wehrmacht near Mt. Cassino.

A truck pulled up in front of the house and the men who were back from the front, either because of injury or for a brief rest, helped load the carcasses into the waiting vehicle. They waited while a few stragglers arrived at the house, one woman with some chickens slung over her shoulder, another with a shank of beef. The butcher, Signor Pipitone, sat next to the driver of the truck and they pulled out in the direction of his shop. Even with the carcasses removed, their scent lingered, and my stomach turned.

Suddenly, I wasn't hungry anymore.

Becher, Wolff's second-in-command, approached me. Colonel Wolff was at the front now, and in his absence, Becher had taken over the job of putting together food for soldiers. When he had gathered it, he would go to the front and Wolff would come back. Becher spoke sharply to everyone, and it was no wonder that his men obeyed him quickly. Now, he turned his eyes to me.

"Benedetta. You have two pigs, no?"

I nodded.

"Bring them out front."

My heart sank, even though I had known this time would come.

I walked outside, past the bread oven, then around back to the barn, which sat about a hundred yards from the house. A low stone wall circled the entire area, leading up to the edge of the forest.

A chicken coop ran off the back of the barn, and a pen for the pigs jutted out from the main entrance. The chicken coop had been in disrepair for some years, but the pigs had done well.

A lean-to provided shade for the pigs now standing along the fence. The wind generally blew the other way, so the smell was not bad. They squealed when they saw me, expecting a treat of garbage from the kitchen.

As I got closer I heard a strange sound. It seemed to be coming from the pen, but farther back. When I got to the fence, I saw the piglet cowering behind his mother. We had thought that she was pregnant, but sometimes it was hard to tell. Papa would be very happy, under other circumstances, to have a new member of the family. But the little piglet's short life was about to come to an abrupt end.

I looked back toward the house. This was going to be harder than I thought.

I walked through the main doors and entered the pen through the small trapdoor beneath the lean-to. I had a stick in my hand and used it to push the adult pigs toward the other side of the pen. I then scooped up the piglet and held him, squirming, in my arms. He was heavy for being only a few days old.

A thought came to my mind and I quickly stepped back into the shed. Becher had asked for two pigs.

The barn had really become a catchall. It was now a workshop, tack room, and storage shed all rolled into one. Along one wall were the animal stalls, now empty. The other wall held a primitive workbench with a few rusted tools hanging in front of it. There were odd scraps of leather, nails, and piles of junk. In the barn's far corner, farthest from the house, was another trapdoor leading to the chicken pen.

My eye was drawn to the space between the workbench and the trapdoor leading to the chicken coop. At one point, my father had built another, smaller coop along this back wall. The door to the inside coop was long and rectangular, the kind that you lifted up, and the door itself had a hook in the center. When you lifted the door up, you slid the hook through an eye screw that was screwed into the wall above it. When the door was hooked, it hung open while the chickens were fed. At one time, it had always remained open and there had been a narrow path along the wall, bordered by chicken wire, that allowed the chickens to go back and forth.

It hadn't been used in years, as we had given up raising chickens. Since my mother's death, in fact. It had always been her job. The only bird remaining in the outdoor coop was our rooster, and he was getting very old.

I raised the door to the chicken coop and looked inside. It was empty for the most part, just some scrap tools and a bucket with a hole in it. I placed the piglet inside, then closed the door. I went back to the pigpen, where the piglet's mother snorted indignantly and questioned me with her eyes. I couldn't meet her gaze and scooped up some ears of corn as well as some hay. There was also a bucket of mixed grain. I put the bucket and corn inside the coop with the piglet. Not knowing when I would be able to come back, I thought it better to give it the whole thing than risk having it die from starvation. I put a bucket of water in there with him and then closed the door, locking it with the crude latch my father had probably fashioned by hand.

I slid a giant, cracked washtub and an old hand plow harness in front of the door. Pressing my ear against the wooden door, I struggled to hear any sound, but there was nothing. I knew it would be complete darkness inside. What I didn't know was what it would do to the piglet, if he survived at all. But then, I thought, wasn't that true for all of us?

I walked back through the shed, shutting the main door tightly. Snapping the pigs on their bottoms with my stick, I eventually herded them up the long path to the house. Becher was nowhere to be seen when I rounded the front corner with them.

Schlemmer emerged from the house with another German soldier. They each had a piece of bread in their hand. Schlemmer looked at me, but his face showed no emotion, just a cold, blank stare.

The other soldier said something in German and Schlemmer's eyes fell on the pigs, now shuffling around the yard in confusion, grunting their displeasure with the whole situation.

Becher came from the house. He barked orders to Schlemmer and the other soldier, who promptly pulled long knives from their belts. Leaving the pigs behind, I moved toward the house, then stood next to Becher, watching.

Schlemmer and the other soldier each got hold of a pig and slid their knives under the animals' throats. I tried to close my eyes but I couldn't. I wanted to see the Germans kill the pigs that my father and I had raised. I wanted to see these men spill blood on the ground not more than twenty yards from my house.

The two soldiers moved as one, cutting upward quickly and smoothly, then stepping back as each pig took several tentative steps, swaying as the blood spurted from their severed jugular veins. The pigs sank to their knees and then dropped in the dirt, blood pooling around them. As I raised my eyes from the pigs, I found myself looking directly into Schlemmer's grinning face. His teeth were yellow and his face was flushed.

"We will eat these now, Benedetta," said Becher. "Please prepare them immediately."

I nodded numbly and went inside the house.

CHAPTER TEN

—

On the sixth day of my father's absence a rumor made its way through the village that Bishop Frugazzi was on his way. In the larger province of Frosinone, Bishop Frugazzi was the highest-ranking clergy. To have a priest of his stature come to our village was an honor, and a cause for celebration.

He was coming, ostensibly, to meet the Germans, as well as to bless the village and pray for our safety as the war raged on all around us.

By lunchtime, the rumor had grown to fact: The bishop would indeed be arriving in Casalvieri at noon. The rumor was confirmed by Colonel Wolff, who called me to discuss the matter.

"You've heard of the man?" he asked.

"Oh, yes," I said. "This is an honor for all of us in Casalvieri."

He smiled. "Your faith is admirable, Benedetta."

For some reason, I didn't think he admired my strong Catholic faith at all. There seemed to be a touch of mockery in his smile.

"Here is a bottle of wine," he said, handing it to me. "Please serve it to us at lunch."

"To who?" I asked.

"Don Frugazzi will be coming here for lunch."

"Here?"

"Here. Is there a problem?"

"No, no," I said. The fear I had been feeling since the Germans' arrival was now replaced with a nervous excitement. Without saying another word to Wolff, I rushed to the kitchen and retrieved the best jar of tomatoes I could find, the one with the biggest chunks, and immediately set out to make Bishop Frugazzi the best spaghetti lunch he had ever had.

The freshest garlic, onion, and olive oil, with chunks of pork, all went into the rich sauce. The thickest pasta I could find was boiled. I had never worked so quickly or so efficiently in the kitchen in my life. My hands flew with a speed and precision I didn't know I possessed.

The best tablecloth, last used for the wake after my mother's funeral, went on the table. From a felt-lined wooden box came the few pieces of mismatched fine silverware that we reserved for special occasions.

While everything cooked, I hurried to Zizi Checcone's, holding my dress up so I could run as fast as my feet would fly. Iole and Emidio were playing together in her yard. They saw me coming and raced to meet me.

"Benny, what's wrong?" Iole asked, her big brown eyes wide with anticipated fright.

I laughed. "Nothing! Just the opposite!"

Emidio was clinging to my dress.

"Father Frugazzi—the bishop—is coming to our house for lunch!" I told them.

They looked at me, clearly not grasping the seriousness of the occasion.

"Come with me—you can meet him and help serve lunch," I said. "Papa will be so happy to know how well we took care of the bishop. This is an important occasion for the Carlesimo family!"

"This is an important occasion for all of Casalvieri!" Zizi Checcone said, emerging from the front door of the house. She began to brush Iole's hair with her fingers and straighten Emidio's shirt and collar, then turned to frantically trying to smooth out the wrinkles in my dress.

We raced back to the house and I sent Iole and Emidio upstairs to change. I tested the pasta to make sure it was right, biting a noodle in half to see that it felt firm but not crisp, soft but not soggy. *Al dente.*

The sound of voices reached the kitchen, and soon Wolff led Bishop Frugazzi into the kitchen. The bishop was a short, wide man, balding, with horn-rimmed glasses. He was dressed in black and was sweating profusely.

"This is Benedetta Carlesimo," Wolff said. "She's taking good care of us."

The bishop's chubby hand took mine and he kissed it, then kissed both of my cheeks. "Ah, Benedetta, the blessed," he said. "What a beautiful name, and such a beautiful girl!"

He turned to Wolff. "You are lucky to have such a beautiful *zoccola.*"

I blushed at the word, which means a woman of ill repute. I was certain that I hadn't heard right, that the bishop hadn't just called me that horrible name. I then busied myself with the food. Iole and Emidio came downstairs and were introduced to the bishop. They helped me finish setting the table while Wolff and Bishop Frugazzi began talking.

"How goes the . . . effort, Colonel Wolff?" the bishop began.

"Excellent, excellent."

"Good."

"We are pushing, the Americans are trying to reach us, but we throw them back, almost effortlessly," Wolff said. To me, however, his voice didn't sound as certain as his words.

"The big guns . . . ?" the bishop asked.

"Yes, the big guns are too much for them."

Bishop Frugazzi drained his glass and motioned for me to refill it, which I did.

"They will soon give up," said the bishop. "They lose too many men."

Wolff nodded in agreement.

"I hear about the American losses," continued Bishop Frugazzi. "Word from my parishioners is that the southern slope of Mt. Cassino is covered with dead Americans."

"Our men are good fighters," said Wolff.

I placed the bowl of spaghetti on the table. The bishop served himself, then pushed the bowl across to Wolff, who was clearly not as experienced with pasta. He awkwardly heaped a pile of the pasta onto his plate.

"And how are your people?" asked Wolff, struggling to wrap noodles around his fork. He watched Bishop Frugazzi use his spoon to hold the pasta while twirling the fork, but this technique was clearly beyond the German's reach.

"They are good," the bishop said, obviously distracted by the food in front of him. The bishop drained his glass again and I refilled it. The bottle was almost empty. "They say the Germans treat them well."

"We want it that way, Your Excellency. We are not here to hurt anyone." Wolff paused a moment. "At least not any innocent civilians."

"It shows, Colonel Wolff."

Bishop Frugazzi heaped even more pasta onto his plate. "There are shortages, of course," he said. "But that is to be expected during times of war."

"Some things cannot be avoided," Wolff agreed.

"Many villages are short on food already. But our people are survivors."

"The strong survive."

"Those who survive were meant to survive," the bishop said knowingly.

Just then, Iole retrieved the empty bread basket from the table and was passing the bishop when he reached out and grasped one of her pigtails. He jerked quickly but firmly and Iole let out a small yelp, like a dog whose tail was just stepped on.

I saw shocked tears leap into Iole's eyes.

"More wine!" called the bishop, holding up his empty glass. I fought down my anger and emptied the rest of the bottle into his glass. It occurred to me that the bishop might be drunk.

As I finished filling his glass, his arm snaked around me and pulled me closer to him. "Ah, Colonel Wolff, you have picked a fine place for your headquarters. All the comforts of home, no?" he said, shooting Wolff a sly wink.

Wolff did not smile. His eye caught mine and he sent me a message. "Benedetta," he said, "start cleaning the dishes. The bishop and I will go outside for a cigar."

I jerked myself away from the bishop. "He could use the fresh air," I said to Wolff. "Maybe he will remember his manners."

Everyone fell silent in the house. And then the bishop laughed out loud at me.

Wolff led him out the door and Iole came to me, wiping her eyes dry with the backs of her hands. "I'm sorry, Benny," she said. "But it hurt."

I grabbed her by her shoulders and brought her to my chest, then pushed her back and looked into her eyes.

"You have nothing—absolutely nothing—to be sorry for," I said.

I hugged her again, wondering if during the war nothing would remain sacred.

Not even God.

CHAPTER ELEVEN

—

Several more days passed with no word from or of my father. The nights, of course, were the toughest; four, maybe five hours of sleep each night were all I could manage.

The days had already begun to fall into a routine. I got out of bed with the first hint of light—I was usually awake anyway—and went down to the kitchen, where Zizi Checcone was already starting to prepare food for the day.

I heard one soldier talking about the shortages of meat, gasoline, and other items related to the war, but the Germans seemed to have plenty of flour readily available. If their vehicles ran out of gas, at least they'd have plenty of bread to eat while they walked. We usually started by making the bread dough, then I would go outside, build the fire, come back inside, get the loaves, then take them back out to the oven. There, I put them inside on racks, then closed the big doors and sealed them with clay.

Zizi Checcone would typically go back to her house after the initial morning work was done, and I would move on to the day's laundry. Sometimes I brought water from the well in a huge pot and built a fire in the fire pit out front. Other times, I would carry the bundles to some springs about a half mile from the house. There, I would scrub the clothes and pound them gently with rocks until they were clean. It was hard, dull work that kept my hands occupied and let my mind drift.

I thought about everything while I worked, mostly my mother and father, the early times when we were all together and the house was loud with laughter and love. Things had not returned to normal, and they never would, I knew that. But one day I hoped we would, as a family, learn how to laugh again.

When I got home, my father was standing in front of the house, next to a truck, talking to the driver. Even from a distance I could tell that he had lost much weight; as I got closer, I could see the lines on his face looked deeper, and the folds of skin seemed to hang more loosely.

I hurried to meet him and he turned to me, but then I froze. My father's clothes were covered with blood. My heart jumped into my throat, and I looked for bandages, waiting for him to fall into my arms. Instead, he picked me up and hugged me with all his strength. Looking over his shoulders, I saw the explanation.

The truck bed was literally awash with blood. Dried rivers of red made their way to pools in the back of the truck. The sidewalls of the truck bed were streaked with splashes of dried blood, slowly turning black.

I closed my eyes at the sight, disgusted but at the same time gloriously happy that the blood was not my father's.

"Benny."

Tears were streaming down my face.

"Benny."

Papa pulled me away from him and I felt his thumbs on my cheeks, wiping away the tears.

"What does a man have to do around here to get a cup of coffee?" he asked.

I laughed as he set me down, then I took his hand and led him inside the house.

He sat heavily at the table, a deep sigh escaping his lips. Inside, he looked smaller and paler. I poured him a cup of coffee.

"I'm going to get Emidio and Iole," I said.

"No," my father said. "Wait."

He pushed a chair away from the table with his foot and indicated that I should sit.

"Tell me what is happening here," he said.

I told him how my days had fallen into a routine, and what that routine was. He nodded as I spoke, sipping his coffee. I then told him about the visit from the bishop, leaving out the part about how Bishop Frugazzi had made Iole cry, and how he had put his arm around me.

Papa's face beamed with pride as I described how the bishop had dined in our house, at the very same table where he was now sitting. He seemed particularly happy when I described the meal I had made, and how much the holy man had enjoyed it.

"Good," he said. "Good."

He asked if there was anything else he should know and I said that there wasn't. He asked if the Germans were treating me well and I said yes.

I realized I'd forgotten about the pigs, so I told him that they had been slaughtered, then, whispering, told him about how I had hidden the piglet in the indoor chicken coop and that we were secretly feeding him with the few scraps I could manage to sneak out to him.

Papa laughed. "That's my Benedetta. You're just like your mother."

We both paused briefly at the mention of her.

The smile disappeared from my father's face and I decided to change the subject.

"How are you doing, Papa?"

He looked at me, a strange flash of anger taking away the sadness in his eyes. Papa stood and walked into the other rooms of the house before returning to the table.

"I am going to try to escape the front, Benny," he said.

"What . . . how . . . ?"

"It is too dangerous. If I don't do something now . . ." He shrugged.

"But they won't let you . . ."

"If an Italian man disappears during the battle, the Germans assume he was killed or captured. It's only if they actually see us running away that they try to shoot us. And even then, they might not want to waste a bullet on us."

He paused, then added, "I can die trying or I can just die," he said.

I said nothing. I felt dizzy.

"The Germans do not consider us people," Papa said. "We are not human. In their eyes we are lower beings. A step above monkeys. A step below them. They make us do the most dangerous jobs. Hauling artillery and explosives on our backs through rough terrain."

His voice had turned bitterly angry. I reached across the table and took his hands, looking quickly around the room. He lowered his voice. "The Americans are trying to make it up Mt. Cassino," he said. "You can hear the guns booming from here, can't you?"

I nodded.

"But the Germans, they have the big guns above the only pass, the Mignano Gap," Papa said. "The Americans are committing suicide every night. In the morning, the Germans send us out to strip anything of value off the dead Americans. Two days ago, an Italian was shot by a wounded American."

He shook his head and I refilled his coffee cup.

"There are dogs everywhere on that side of the mountain," Papa said. "There isn't enough food on that side either, where the Americans are. The villagers are caught in the middle, so their dogs run free. They are feasting on the Americans, tearing flesh from the corpses that haven't had time to rot."

I shuddered at the image.

"Listen to me, Benny," my father said, taking my hands in his. "Before you get Emidio and Iole, remember, I am going to try to get away from there. Away from them. You must be strong, stronger than ever, Benny. I'm counting on you."

He sat back in his chair, the dark circles under his eyes making him look even more exhausted.

I left him sitting there, looking into his cup of coffee, the weight of the war resting heavily on his sloping shoulders.

CHAPTER TWELVE

—

In the morning, my father left with the Germans, naturally, for the front. We kissed him good-bye at the front door. Iole and Emidio were in tears, as was I. He hugged Signora Checcone, which surprised me, and then walked out with the tread of a condemned man. Seeing him climb back into the truck sank my heart like a stone. The only hope I could cling to was that he would somehow manage to escape, somehow manage to find a mountain.

It had taken me quite awhile to get used to the Germans' big guns booming at night. They kept me awake until I finally got the best sleep aid of all: complete and total fatigue.

Things had started to change, though. Gradually, the explosions began to occur sporadically throughout the day; now it seemed like the big guns were firing nonstop. It didn't take a military expert to figure out that the Americans were trying even harder to capture Mt. Cassino, to wipe out the enemy that had dug in like a weed and refused to be yanked out, the dark force that had killed so many of their friends and maybe even family.

These mountains were strange to the Americans and the Germans, but had been home to my family for generations. I wondered if the families of those who died would ever see the hard ground upon which so much of their children's blood was spilled. I wondered if the families had ever even heard of the region of Frosinone.

After lunch on the day my father left—a meager lunch consisting of thin menestra and dry, crumbling bread—I walked and tried to shake the image he'd left with me of roads strewn with dead bodies being torn apart by wild dogs. It made me wonder: If Papa did manage to find a mountain, would he really be safe even there?

When I got back home, I put on a happy face that felt like it had no right being there, like wearing a colorful dress to a funeral.

In the kitchen, Iole was helping Zizi Checcone peel acorns.

"Benny!" Iole cried. "You're just in time to help us!"

Zizi Checcone smiled and patted Iole on the head. "Your little sister here sure knows her way around the kitchen, Benedetta."

"Really? It's a side of her I believe I've yet to see," I said, giving Iole a playful pinch on the arm.

"Very funny," Iole said, sticking out her tongue at me. I made a grab to catch it between my fingers but she sucked it back in.

"What are you doing with all these acorns?" I asked. "Trying to starve out the squirrels?"

"Making bread," Iole said, like she had some great secret she was dying for me to ask about.

As I watched, Zizi Checcone painstakingly cracked open an acorn and pulled the small portion of "meat" from its shell. She gave the thumbnail-sized chunk to Iole, who then placed it on a chopping board. Iole took a small tenderizing hammer with a milled face and pounded the acorn meat until it was pulverized into something resembling a miniature pancake.

"It's an old recipe, Benny, and a terrible one at that," Zizi Checcone explained. "But the word is that food shortages are getting worse everywhere. We've got to start finding ways to conserve the food that we do have. These acorns will make a bread that is impossible to eat—unless you are starving. Even then it won't taste good, but it will keep you alive." Like so many Italian women, Zizi Checcone tended to think the worst was going to happen. It was an attitude my mother had shied away from. She had always been by nature a happy, positive person. But now, with the war raging, I didn't think it was such a bad thing to think the worst. The worst would probably turn out to be reality.

The small pile of crushed acorn in Iole's mixing bowl did little to convince me that bread would actually come out of all this.

"What's next?" I asked.

"We add salt and a little bit of olive oil, and then we bake it."

"Tell her about the dandelions!" Iole insisted, beaming.

"Dandelions?" I asked, raising an eyebrow.

"Emidio is getting more acorns, and all the dandelions he can find," Iole informed me.

"What will you do with the dandelions, Zizi Checcone?"

"The leaves have some nutrients, not much but some. Again, terrible if you've got plenty of food on the table, close to edible if you're starving. Some people even use them to make a crude wine."

"Maybe we'll all get drunk and not even notice that we're starving," Iole offered.

I laughed at Iole, then smiled at Zizi Checcone's ingenuity.

"I know, Benedetta," she said. "Not a dish the great chefs in Naples would serve to their worst customer, but it can help us survive."

"Let me help . . ." I said.

Zizi Checcone pointed to a small burlap bag. Inside was a considerable cache of fresh dandelions. I set to work, pulling the roots off each plant, followed by the stem and flower, if it had any. Once

I had a sizable amount of leaves, I threw them into a small pan of oil, garlic, and a little bit of water. They were to be sautéed.

The back door opened and Emidio walked in with another burlap bag over his shoulders. He held out his hand.

"Look what I found, everyone!" he exclaimed.

It was a hand grenade.

CHAPTER THIRTEEN

—

The bread oven looked more like a small shed. It had about as much room as a tiny closet. The fire pit was underneath, and above it, several racks for the bread. It was made of stone and sealed with clay. I once tried to estimate how many loaves of bread had been made in this oven, but found the task impossible. For starters, I didn't know how old the oven was; it had been here before either my mother or father had been born.

I opened the oven door and pulled out the wooden rack upon which four loaves of bread sat, their golden crusts still glowing over the red embers below. The scent of fresh-baked bread washed over me; it was the best smell in the world and made bearable the sometimes mundane task of making bread, baking it, retrieving it from the oven, and starting the whole process again the very next day.

The advertisement was deceptive. I knew this batch, made of a mixture of Zizi Checcone's acorn surprise with more traditional ingredients, smelled like good bread but tasted more like burlap. I would have to use the opposite of the expression used by so many mothers to get children to eat food that tasted good but looked bad: "Iole! Emidio! Eat it! It's not how it tastes; it's how it looks!"

I joked that if we didn't eat the bread, we could use it to scrub the pots after dinner.

I was almost glad to eat this kind of bread, because it meant most of the Germans were eating it, too. And I felt there was some justice there—not much, but a little. They too would understand the challenge of the moment: to stretch the ingredients as far as they could go while preserving the food's ability to sustain. The first thing to suffer? Taste. Who cared what it tasted like as long as it filled the belly?

Becher had told me earlier in the day that a convoy from the front would be returning, carrying the dead, the wounded, and what remained of the living. When I saw the trucks pull up, the living and the wounded looked dead, their eyes staring off, oblivious to the fact that the truck had stopped. Sometimes the driver would have to tell them, gently at first, to get out, but some of them needed to be shouted at. And then they would jump, startled, as if their brains were still back on the bloody slope of Mt. Cassino.

It had been several weeks since my father left for the front and now I desperately hoped he would return, despite his plan to escape to a mountain. I wanted to see him, to hold him, to know that he was alive and well. It had been too long to go without him; Iole's and Emidio's questions about what he was doing were becoming more frequent and insistent. It was tiresome to have to lie to them day in and day out during a time like this, when we needed each other the most.

Back in the house, I poured the last of the espresso from the small copper-lined pot next to the hearth. It was weak and watery; I had used just enough of the beans to get a hint of the flavor and not much more. As I sat at the table, thoughts of the war went through my mind. Images of the barren fields, homes empty except for the women and children, Italian men dying on the front in a war they wanted nothing to do with. It was too much to comprehend. The life of the village before the war had been hard, and not just for me because of the loss of my mother. Many families hated it in the mountains, dreamed of going to Naples, Rome, or north to the wealthier cities. It was a life from which to escape, not to enjoy. But now, everyone longed for that previous life. It was like a youth that had ended abruptly, even for the oldest men and women of Casalvieri.

And for what was all this suffering and death? The Germans would not win the war. I had watched Wolff and Becher listen to their precious radio late at night and hang their heads afterward. They did not look like triumphant generals of a conquering army. They looked like parents hovering around the deathbed of their child.

No, the Germans would not win. They would simply return to their country and all they would succeed in doing here was to destroy families, villages, and, temporarily, a way of life. But like weeds, everything would grow back eventually. The Germans would no more be remembered than a bad storm that knocked down some trees.

At least, I hoped that would be the case.

The sound of a rumbling engine drew closer and I set down my cup, then moved to the window next to the front door. A truck came slowly into view and somehow I knew my father was not on it. It stopped in front of the house and Wolff swung down clumsily from the front passenger seat, his bulk not permitting him to move gracefully. He did not look back at his men in the truck but came directly to the house.

I stepped away from the window and stood in the open doorway.

A few men jumped out from the back of the truck bed. They walked silently away in different directions, averting their gazes. I recognized most of them, had served them bread, but for some reason they did not wish to look me in the eye.

"Benedetta, come sit with me," Wolff said.

Wolff put his arm around my shoulders and led me back into the house. He sat me down at the table and I knew what was coming.

"There's only one way to say these things."

I started crying, the first tears pooling at the edges of my eyes and then dropping down my cheek.

"Your father is dead."

The words struck like hammers on hollow wood inside my head. They were words I had heard before, spoken by my father. Except that time, it was about my mother.

I sobbed unashamedly.

"Benedetta, he and another man were in a truck, going back to the front to get more wounded. There was an explosion . . ." He held his hands out as if to say there was nothing he could do. "There is no doubt."

It answered all of the questions but one, and I knew then that it was a question I had to ask.

"Did you find his . . . did you see him?" I asked.

He pulled a bundle from a bag at his feet and I recoiled, screaming, imagining body parts inside. Seeing my father's hand or foot would be too much.

"No! No! Benedetta, calm down," he said, and quickly pulled an article of clothing from the bag. "Is this your father's?"

It was Papa's shirt, covered in blood and nearly torn to shreds, but still recognizable.

"We found it along with other . . . parts. There was no way he could have survived, Benny. They both died quickly and painlessly. I'm sorry."

I ripped the shirt from Wolff's grip and hugged it to my chest. Anger ignited inside me at the sound of the apology.

"Sorry? Sorry? You are not sorry!" I yelled and jumped to my feet. The chair flew backward and toppled over with a loud crash. "We are not people to you! You think of us as mules!" My face was hot with fury. "When one of us dies, all it means to you is that another precious German will live to fight another day!"

Wolff looked at me coolly, almost appraisingly.

I raced up the stairs and flung myself on my bed, still hugging my father's shirt. I don't know how long I cried, but when I finally stopped, it was dark and the house was silent once again.

A gusty wind picked up outside, sending small pebbles bouncing off the side of the house. If Papa had orchestrated the accident, the explosion, would he really have left his shirt? Or was that part of the plan? Did the men who escaped to the mountains ever try to fake their deaths? I'd never heard of such a thing. Papa was a slow, steady man, not given to great dreams or revolutionary ideas. He was a good man, but a conventional one. I did not see him planning something so elaborate and dangerous.

Hours later, almost with no conscious decision made, I walked back downstairs into the kitchen. My feet were heavy, and I felt like I was floating above myself, seeing the top of my head, my slow shuffle.

I opened a far cabinet and reached in the back, behind many plates and glasses. My hands closed around an object and I walked back into the middle of the room.

The grenade felt heavy in my hands.

When Emidio had come in the back door we were all in shock, but I had decided to keep it; why, I don't know. We didn't have any guns in the house, and a kitchen knife was only so useful. It seemed like the right thing to do; after all, hand grenades were for wars.

But right now, I wasn't thinking about self-preservation. I was thinking about revenge. An eye for an eye. A father for a father. A handful of filthy *Germanesi* for one good man. It would be so simple. After the soldiers were fast asleep, I could just walk to their door, open it a crack, pull the grenade's pin, and roll the grenade in.

I hefted the instrument of death in my hand. It was green like an olive, with a thin band of yellow around the top. There was a silver handle along with a pin that I was sure not to touch. The whole thing was much heavier than I thought it would be. At least a pound or two.

It was amazing to me that such force could all be contained in an object of this size. Just like a bullet. I looked at my hand, so thin and so weak compared to this . . . this thing. Muscle, tendon, and bone. They were nothing compared to explosives, gunpowder, and bullets.

Suddenly, I felt my soul, my consciousness, float back down and come back into my body. When it happened, reason came with it.

No, I didn't want to kill anyone.

Germans dying in the Carlesimo house would mean many people in Casalvieri dying also. A grenade like this could set off many other explosions and reactions that would probably kill many more people than this initial blast. Plus, like so many of the Italian men and women in the rugged farming countryside, hope refused to die that somewhere our loved ones were still alive.

I put the grenade back in the cupboard. Iole, Emidio, and Zizi Checcone would be returning soon.

There was food to be made and laundry to be washed.

I got to work.

CHAPTER FOURTEEN

—

When I answered the knock on the door, a flood of warmth swept through me when I saw that it was Lauretta. She didn't say anything at first, just hugged me hard.

I desperately did not want to cry, but I couldn't stop myself. I felt ashamed at displaying so much emotion, but it felt so good to be crushed to her breast, to be patted on the back and have my hair stroked by Lauretta's big, callused hand.

"Benedetta, we are very sorry to hear about your father."

Before I could answer, Iole and Emidio raced down the stairs and gave Lauretta hugs. I turned my face away so they couldn't see my emotions.

Lauretta caught my eye and an exchange was made. The little ones had not been told about Papa, and would not be told until I heard from the men in the mountains that Papa had not been seen. Only then would I be truly convinced that he was dead.

"Are these two good little helpers, Benny?" Lauretta asked.

Iole and Emidio looked at me, devilish smiles on their faces, daring me to answer in the negative.

"When they want to be," I said, raising my eyebrows at them as if to say, "Care to disagree?"

She looked around the house, and I assured her that we were alone for the moment. Colonel Wolff had left in the morning before I could speak to him, which I chose to accept as a sign that I would not be punished for my outburst. I was not sure how I would handle facing him again. I would apologize if I had to. I needed to take care of my family now. The Germans could be ruthless and usually were, so I saw no good in putting ourselves in any more danger. There was plenty to go around for everyone.

Zizi Checcone opened the door behind me.

"Lauretta Fandella! How are you?"

"We are doing well, Signora Checcone."

"How are your parents?"

"Mother is busy, but we are managing to make ends meet."

"Good, good," said Zizi Checcone.

"Benny," Lauretta began. "Can you go for a walk with me?"

I started to say no, thinking of the bread that still needed to be baked as well as the laundry to be washed, but before I could reply, Zizi Checcone answered for me.

"Go, Benedetta. Walk with your friend."

"But there is bread to be baked . . ."

"I have been baking bread all my life; I think I can do it one more time without your help," Zizi Checcone said. "Go. You need to get out and talk to someone your own age before you go crazy here."

"Thank you, Signora Checcone." Iole and Emidio stood looking at me, silently asking if they could come along, too. I gave them each a squeeze. "You two be good while I'm gone." I just couldn't stand keeping things from them much longer, and Lauretta would be someone with whom I could speak openly.

"I'll be back in an hour or two," I said.

Zizi Checcone nodded and put her arms around my brother and sister. Lauretta and I left the house and began walking, silently at first, out of town, with an unspoken agreement to head for a large outcropping near the peak of the mountain just outside Casalvieri. It was a favorite place for the young people of the village to go. Many families, before the war, went there for picnics. Now, it was all but abandoned.

It took us almost half an hour to get there, and on the way, I asked Lauretta if she had heard anything about her father, and if he had joined a band of *ribelli*.

"I'm not allowed to talk about it," Lauretta said firmly. "But I can tell you that he is keeping busy in the mountains."

"Has he heard anything about my father?"

Lauretta looked at me. "I was wondering if you had considered that possibility."

"That Papa didn't die?"

"A lot of men have disappeared from the front," Lauretta said. "The Germans assume most of them died, but probably suspect some ran away. But we know the truth—that many of them end up in the mountains, where it is awful, but safe."

I was silent, still imploring her to answer my question.

"We have not gotten word from the *ribelli* for several days now," Lauretta said. "Hopefully we will again soon. I will ask about your father, Benedetta."

"Thank you."

We had made it to the top of the peak, where a small clearing had been made well back from the tree line. There was a cool breeze up here, and from the viewpoint, looking north, away from Mt. Cassino and the front, everything looked deceptively peaceful. A hawk slowly cruised below us, hunting its prey.

We sprawled out on the green grass, facing each other.

"I hope this will all be over soon," I said.

"This is terrible," Lauretta agreed. "No men! Even the Germans are too occupied, so to speak!"

We both burst into a fit of laughter.

"If our men weren't fighting the Germans, they'd be fighting over those things," I said, pointing to her breasts.

She cupped them and looked them over, as if appraising diamonds. "I need a man to plant a flag between them and claim them as rightfully Italy's. Our national treasures!"

We both collapsed laughing again.

"This war better not last too much longer, Benedetta. Or we'll be old maids and too late."

"I hope we live to be old maids."

"I don't," Lauretta said. "I'd rather die young, beautiful, and the object of some man's lust than a dried-up old hag."

Then we heard the explosions.

The sound was incredibly loud, and we both jumped to our feet. Even though we knew they had to be several miles away, the immediacy of the explosions caught us off guard.

Gradually, we began to hear the drone of engines. Lauretta and I looked at each other in fear and wonderment, then turned to the tree line behind us as the sound of the engines got closer. I judged the trees were too far away for us to make it to them in time, and as if to support my guesswork, out of the clouds directly in front of us flew an American bomber with three fighter escorts.

The sound was so loud that we both clasped our hands over our ears.

Suddenly, one of the fighters broke from its formation and came straight at us. I could feel the eyes of the pilot upon us, imagined the muzzles of the machine guns located in the plane's wings pointed right at me, the bullets ready to rip our bodies to shreds.

We stood frozen in terror as the plane came nearer and nearer.

Then the plane tipped from side to side.

"He's waving!" Lauretta yelled at me and she swung her hand over her head, in a wide sweeping motion, waving back.

The last thing I saw as the plane rocketed off was a quick glimpse of the American pilot twisted back in his seat in his leather helmet, his goggles catching the sun as he waved his hand at us.

And he was smiling.

Lauretta looked at me and then me at her and without a word, we raced back to Casalvieri.

CHAPTER FIFTEEN

—

B enedetta, this wine is excellent."
Colonel Wolff was seated at the kitchen table. His uniform
jacket was unbuttoned at the collar, his cap was off, and a letter,
along with a bottle of wine and two glasses, sat on the table.

"Thank you."

He caught the look in my eye, heard the unfeeling tone in my
voice. Maybe he could even sense the hatred.

"I know it is hard, Benedetta. But your father is making more
of this," he said, raising his glass, "and drinking more of this in
Heaven right now."

I said nothing, not wanting to cry again. And it wasn't even that
I wanted to cry out of sadness or pain, as much as it was frustration,
not knowing. What was worse: mourning the loss of a parent, or
not knowing if you should mourn because you don't know if that
parent is dead?

Instead, I chose to focus on the sadness. The Lord knew I was
familiar with that, and I did it because I didn't want Wolff to see

through my emotions to my frustration. He wanted to see a girl in mourning over the loss of her father.

"Join me."

He picked up the remaining glass and poured a small amount of the white wine. I picked up the glass, took it to the hearth where a pot of water sat, and added a healthy amount. When I sat back down, Wolff again raised his glass.

"Health," he said.

"*Saluté*," I responded, wanting to throw the wine in his face. How dare he toast me with wine made by the man he ordered to his death? I should bring a knife and ram it into his black heart.

We sipped, and I felt the wine roll on my tongue as its sweet flavor blossomed briefly, then faded into a warmly satisfying afterthought. I said a silent prayer to God that Papa would return and have a chance to taste this wine.

"Tell me how you make this," Wolff said.

He drained his glass with one long pull then refilled it. Once his glass was full, his free hand absentmindedly strayed to the letter on the table next to him, his fingers alternately tapping, caressing, and circling the envelope.

"Well, first of course are the grapes."

"Grown around here, I assume?"

"Yes, in the Abruzzio region, west of here. That's where the best grapes are. After Papa selects the plumpest, juiciest ones, he brings them to the back of the house and puts them in the big wooden tub."

Colonel Wolff listened intently as I described the tub, about how it had a giant screw and circular fitted wooden top that, when cranked, slowly lowers itself onto the grapes, squashing them. Nearly every house in the village had something similar. He interrupted to ask questions, clarifying certain points. I told him about when the juice runs out of the tub, it is funneled into a wooden keg where sugar, as well as water and a few secret ingredients, are added, and then it ferments for a period, after which the excess is filtered out.

"That's it?"

"No, this process is repeated, along with periodic stirring to mingle the flavors, until the wine tastes rich and smooth. Usually the entire process takes several months. Longer, depending on how long you are willing to wait."

"It's so good, very different from the dark beers and ales I drink back in Germany."

"Which do you like better?"

He laughed. "Ah, that is simple. I am a German. As much as I like your wine, it will be at best a close second." He drained yet another glass and promptly refilled it.

"You see how people are different, Benedetta? As much as we live here among you, we will never be Italian and you will never be German."

Thank God, I thought to myself. I would rather be condemned to Hell than to be a German.

He gestured with his arm in a vague sweeping motion. "We do not belong here."

His words had begun to slur slightly.

"You cannot take people from their home and expect them to adjust. Habits are too well ingrained. Look at Schlemmer," Wolff said. "This war has completely destroyed him, and he is still a relatively young man. People can experience different things; they can even grow. But they cannot change. Not in a significant way."

His eyes had a far-off look that slowly dissipated as he focused on me.

"To answer your question," he said, "I prefer the dark beer of my . . . homeland."

Was there a slight sneer, a faint tinge of disgust at the mention of "homeland"?

"We Germans are a stubborn people. But you can see that, can't you?" He smiled. "Take my wife, for example. There's a proud German, a tribute to her race." Now there was definite sarcasm there, with a pinch of bitterness thrown in.

"Yes, she will never change, I am sure of that," he said, his voice thickening. "Of course, why change something when it's already perfect, right?"

He took another deep drink of wine.

"Always striving, always working toward a pointless goal. Society. She wants to have more than everyone else, be more important, flaunt money more than the people she allows to know her."

He shook his head, a slow, ponderous movement that seemed to require great effort. I wondered if I looked closely enough at the small veins in his cheeks if I could actually see the wine working its way through them.

"She's leaving me, you know. After the war." He slid the letter out of the envelope and looked at it closely.

"Why?" I asked.

"Listen to this," he said, opening the letter and reading from it. "'Each and every person has a potential that I believe is predetermined. It is a barrier. While we have risen together, I feel, sadly, that you, Hermann, will soon begin your descent. I, on the other hand, am being lifted higher by a power I did not know I had, did not know even existed.'"

He laughed mirthlessly and closed the letter.

"She goes on to say she's leaving me for a textile manufacturer."

My glass was empty, and I poured a healthy amount of wine in, this time not watering it down.

"War changes everything," I said.

"But that's just it, Benedetta. From the minute I met her I knew what kind of woman she was," he said. "I even knew this day would come. I married a thought struggling to be an ideal. Whose fault is it that I am now forced to watch it fall short?"

He leaned back in his chair and his eyes bored into me.

"But you know what's really funny?"

I shook my head.

"She thinks that I'm the one who has fallen short." He leaned back in his chair and set his glass on the letter. A bead of perspiration trickled down the glass and darkened a circle onto the paper.

"Have you ever been in love?" he asked.

"No."

"Never been a boy who has caught your eye?"

"I work so hard. I don't see many."

"That is a shame. You are a beautiful girl. You have the kind of beauty that is timeless. Eternal. If I were a young man . . ."

I felt his eyes on me, a hungry look on his face. He quickly looked away and his body relaxed. Whatever thought he had, brief as it was, had left.

"But I am not a young man," he finished, then proceeded to drink three glasses of wine. On the fourth glass, he tipped his head back to take in the drink, and he fell backward—Colonel Wolff, the chair, and the wine all crashed in a heap. His glass flew out of his hand and landed behind his head, shattering and spilling wine. As he fell backward, his boot caught the edge of the table and lifted it briefly off the ground, causing the bottle to tip over and roll off the table, where it smashed and sprayed glass in a shower onto the floor.

He struggled to stand up, his face red from the fall, the humiliation, or, more likely, both.

"Are you all right, Colonel Wolff?" I asked, rushing to him, helping him stand up, where he swayed like a sapling blowing in the wind. His arm rested heavily on my shoulder and I put my arm around his waist.

"You didn't tell me the wine was this strong!" he said, then burst into laughter.

"We make it strong," I said. "That way we don't have to drink as much, and it lasts longer."

"That's the second thing tonight that knocked me over," he said, gesturing toward the letter. He reached for the paper and crumpled it up, walked unsteadily to the fireplace, and threw it in among the logs, where it shriveled and blackened.

"Good night," he said, bowing formally at the waist. "It was a wonderful evening. Love, betrayal, and humor. What more could a young girl ask for?"

Lots of things, I thought to myself. But instead, I wished him a good night.

As he trudged toward the stairs, I swept up the glass, the bright pieces twinkling at me. Yet another delicate object smashed by the heavy hands of the *Germanesi*.

There was no doubt in my mind now.

The Germans were going to lose the war.

PART TWO

CHAPTER SIXTEEN

—

December 1944

The hand was clamped tightly over my mouth, tearing me from a dream in which I had run from the Germans and was now hiding in the abandoned chicken coop with the pig, which was trying to eat me. I tried to sit up, but was firmly pushed down. My eyes flew open and I half-expected to see before me the grinning leer of Schlemmer, his eyes watery and mad, wearing the same expression he wore when he killed our pigs in the front yard.

Instead, I saw the alarmed but always kind eyes of Zizi Checcone.

"Shhh!" Her brow was furrowed in concentration, willing me to wake up fully. My body relaxed and she slowly took her hand from my mouth. There was a faint taste, or scent, of tomatoes lingering on my lips.

When she saw that I was alert, she helped me sit up.

"What? What?" I said.

"You must get dressed quickly," she whispered.

"Why?" I said, louder than I intended, and was shushed again, but I barely noticed as I searched frantically for my shoes.

"You're going to the mountain."

"What mountain?" I asked stupidly.

Zizi Checcone rolled her eyes toward the heavens, then pulled a dress over my head. I pushed my arms through the sleeves automatically. It had been a long time since someone had dressed me like this.

"Why?" I tried again.

"I don't know," she answered. "All I know is that you are to go tonight."

I pulled a heavy sweater over my dress, then tied my hair back behind my head.

"Don't ask questions and speak only when spoken to," she said. "You are to walk quickly to the south end of the village, past the church and past the Marciani house. Go to the right side of the road where the footpath starts near the big yellow boulder. Do you know where that is?"

I nodded. By now, my brain was fully awake, and I began to wonder if this had anything to do with Papa.

"Do you know where that is, Benedetta?" Zizi Checcone asked again. I then realized that it was too dark for her to see me nodding yes.

"I know where it is."

"A man will meet you once you start walking up the path. Do what he says—he is risking his life to come and get you."

"Did Papa send him? Does this mean he is alive?" Hope had blossomed in my chest.

"Hush, child! I said I don't know anything."

"What if the Germans see I'm gone?"

"Colonel Wolff said he would not be back for several days, so you should be safe. If he comes back early, we'll say you're at a neighboring village, helping a cousin who is sick."

That made sense to me.

"Be just as careful when you come back," she said, grabbing me by the shoulders and hugging me. Then she shooed me toward the stairs.

My mouth felt dry and my heart pounded as I walked down the stairs to the front door and adjusted to the shock of being awakened from a dead sleep to sneak out of the house in order to climb a mountain. I stopped at the hearth and took a quick drink of water, and then I was out the door and into the cool still of the night.

I walked quickly at first, but then slowed down, realizing that I should look as casual as a girl my age could walking around in the dark at two o'clock in the morning. I doubted there were any Germans out and about at this time of night, but who knew for sure?

The stars were out and a gentle breeze blew. The booming of the distant guns was going strong.

I made my way around the village, walking on the outer paths where soldiers returning from the front would not be traveling. My heart started to slow down as my feet fell into an easy rhythm, and I wished that I had stopped to go to the bathroom before I left. A vision came into my mind of my guide and me being caught by the Germans because I had to stop and pee.

The path narrowed and soon the Marciani house came into view, a low stone structure with a red tiled roof. I passed it quickly as a dog started to bark, and then soon I was beyond it. The path wound its way through trees and thick brush. After several minutes, I realized that I must have missed the entrance to the mountain path marked by the big yellow rock. I backtracked and soon found it. I stood at the path, uncertain. Where was I going? Would I find my father alive or would I have final proof that he was dead? The path into the woods was dark and intimidating. I couldn't see more than a few feet into it.

There was only one way to answer any of my questions, and I plunged into the darkness of the path.

It was a dirt path with large stones sunken deeply and erratically, the kind that make you stub your toe and twist an ankle. The path rose quickly, and I frequently reached out to branches for support, as well as to help pull myself up after a rock tripped me. Soon, though, I fell into an awkward rhythm and my eyes adjusted to the darkness, allowing me to see the more well-worn parts of the path with signs of recent use, and I wasn't stumbling so much. I was even able to pick out small clumps of fresh dirt that signaled the recent presence of a boot.

As I passed a particularly thick stand of trees, a dark shadow silently emerged and stepped in front of me. It was a man, tall and slender, with a black cap on his head that cast a shadow over his face. I froze, hoping to hear a kind voice.

"Benedetta Carlesimo?" he asked softly.

"Yes." My voice sounded small and weak in the darkness of the forest.

"Follow me. It will take two hours. Be as quiet as possible." His voice was so low I couldn't get any feeling for who he was or if I knew him.

With that, he started walking.

We climbed steadily for almost an hour. The trail leveled off at times but always returned to a steep incline that left my thighs burning and my calf muscles aching.

He looked back occasionally to make sure I was still coming, and once in a while paused while I caught my breath. Never once did I hear him even slightly huff with exertion.

At one point, I asked him if my father had sent him. He responded by shushing me.

The walk was torture. I focused on his back, following him like a heifer follows the lead bull through the meadow. When he went right, I went right; when he stepped over something, I stepped over it.

When I thought I could climb no more and was going to pass out, collapse, and roll back down the mountain, my guide suddenly froze in his tracks.

I was so intent on the ground, on putting one foot in front of the other, that my head butted him in the middle of his back and he let out a small *oof.* He regained his footing, turned, and grabbed my arm. I tensed, watching as he strained to listen to the darkness ahead, and I did the same. I heard nothing.

With a grip on my arm that I was certain would leave a bruise, he yanked me off the path into the thick woods just off the trail and pushed me to the ground. He joined me, got down on his belly, and crawled in between and partially under a thick stand of brush, making virtually no noise in the process. He moved slightly to his left and motioned for me to do the same.

I complied, my bare legs scraping the dirt and sticks as a million imaginary bugs, as well as a few very real ones, crawled onto my skin. A memory came to my mind of playing hide-and-seek with Iole, before Emidio was born. I had hidden in the woods just behind the barn, in the dirt, while Iole searched and searched. Finally, when I knew she had given up, I started to get up, and that's when the ants started biting me. My legs, arms, and other delicate parts of my body were on fire. I ran to the house screaming. Mama ran out of the house, eyes wide with fear. She took one look at me, scooped me up, and threw me into the big copper pot she'd been washing clothes in. The pain didn't last long, but the welts were visible proof of my humiliation.

Now, on my stomach next to the strange man, I waited, conscious of any noises and twitching at the slightest feeling on my skin, real or imagined. We waited but I still heard nothing. Just when I thought I could bear it no longer and was ready to whisper to my mountain-climbing companion that this was no place to take a girl, we heard the first, soft sounds of far-off footsteps approaching.

Peering through the branches and leaves, I was able to see a glint of metal, a soft gray of uniform fabric. *Germanesi.* I heard a clunk of leather and the labored breathing of men who had been walking for quite some time. In the darkness above me, I caught a quick glimpse of a rounded silhouette that I recognized to be a German helmet.

They passed haphazardly. This wasn't the single-file marching I'd seen from them on occasion. These soldiers were either stationed here, searching for Italian men who were in hiding, or had been temporarily sent back to Casalvieri for rest.

After they passed, I slowly let my breath out, not realizing that I had been holding it the whole time. When the sounds of their footsteps had disappeared entirely, my body sagged. Almost as if on cue, swarms of mosquitoes and flies found us, attacking every inch of exposed skin with a violent thoroughness. It was time to go. I brought a leg up underneath my body and had started to push up off the ground when my guide's hand shot out, clamping on to my arm. *Great*, I thought. *Now I'll have matching bruises.*

I looked at him, but again, his face was in shadow. I could just see the outline of his nose peeking out, his eyes black hollows trained directly on the path ahead.

Suddenly, anger welled up inside me, and I pulled away from him. Who did he think he was? Easy for him to lie among the biting insects; he had on thick black pants and what looked to be a heavy shirt. His cap even covered his ears from the swarming insects.

Just when I was ready to lay into him, the sound of someone running down the path reached our ears. I held my breath as the man ran toward us. It was a shambling gait, as if one of his legs was shorter than the other. Despite the darkness, I could see what he was doing: He was zipping up his pants.

I turned to look at my guide, wanting to apologize for my foolishness. If he hadn't stopped me, I would be standing right in the middle of the path now. Just in time for the German soldier to run directly into me.

Perhaps sensing my look, my guide turned to me and his eyes glowed from the blackness of the forest. Even in the dark they seemed to shimmer, reminding me of the one time I had been to the

Mediterranean Sea and swum in its brilliantly clear waters. My heart skipped a beat as he focused on me. My palms were suddenly sweaty.

As he stared at me, his eyes suddenly seemed to twinkle, and his lips parted, his clean white teeth gleaming. I think, in the darkness, he was laughing at me.

And then something happened that I would never forget. The German soldier tripped. The sound he made crashing into the ground startled me so much, coming as it did at a time when I was looking into these beautiful blue eyes, that it scared me, startled me, caught me off guard so much that I jerked and a small, soft sound escaped my lips.

The soldier, starting to get up, snapped his head around toward where we were hiding, although a little bit too far to the right. Which worked out perfectly, allowing my guide to burst from the bushes and ram his head into the soldier's stomach before he could react. My guide straightened and his fist swept around in one fluid motion, catching the German flush on the jaw. The element of surprise was entirely on our side. The soldier went down to the ground in a heap.

My guide ripped the rifle from the soldier's hands, jacked open the chamber, and emptied the bullets into his palm. He then threw the rifle farther down the path and heaved the bullets into the forest.

I still hadn't moved.

He reached into the woods and grabbed my arm, then pulled me roughly through the bushes. The small twigs scratched my face and arms.

We ran then, my guide holding me, jerking me along until I could run no more, and then he scooped me up and slung me over his shoulder and ran faster.

I vomited onto his back.

CHAPTER SEVENTEEN

—

Finally, when I thought my kidneys were going to come flying out of my mouth, we branched off from the main path and my guide set me on the ground, then took off walking ahead of me. I followed him along a fainter trail that seemed with every step to be on the verge of disappearing altogether.

Weaving his way through the forest with an obvious ease of familiarity, my guide seemed less preoccupied with remaining silent. He walked with a lightness in his step and from time to time, I thought I heard him whistling. The pauses to listen were also becoming less frequent.

After another ten minutes of walking, we went through deeper woods that spilled us out into a small clearing. The man paused at the forest's edge and whistled softly. Instantly, a soft whistle answered him from the other side of the clearing.

Now there was no thought to hiding as my guide walked quickly, brazenly across the small mountain meadow to a low, long cabin. It looked like the kind of structure used by farmers during slaughter season, or a building used for extra storage.

It was a squat structure made of thick stone and featured a heavy wooden door at the front. A crude roof that looked like it was falling apart hung down in places over the edges of the walls. No smoke curled from the chimney and the windows were black.

He rapped on the door, a series of quick raps followed by a long pause and then one more knock.

The door swung open and a face appeared from the darkness. "Papa!"

His image blurred as the tears came and I felt myself being picked up off the ground, the thick wool of his sweater on my skin, the stubble from his newly grown beard scraping against my cheek. Bright flashes of color exploded inside my closed eyes as the world swirled around me. I sagged in his arms; relief and exhaustion both swept over me in a torrent. It was over. The not knowing, the wondering if I had lost another parent. I wept for myself, for him, and for my mother, with whom I would never have this kind of reunion. He was alive. He was in my arms and I in his. Life was suddenly alive again within me.

Every time I thought the tears were about to stop, they started again. I was dimly aware of others watching, but there was no way I could stop. It had all been too much.

The tears were still coming in ragged sobs and I began to hyperventilate.

"Shhh, Benny. Shhhh." I felt his strong hands on my back, patting me. "Everything's okay." I felt him carry me across the small room and we sat down together. Just when I thought I was calm, a breath would reach out and snatch itself away and I would shudder.

As my eyes adjusted to the dark interior of the cabin, I could make out the primitive cot upon which my father and I were sitting. There were other cots in the room with men either sitting on them or sleeping in them. There were also men in blankets on the floor.

Most of them did not look at us, affording us what little privacy was possible in this setting.

Gradually, the time between sobs grew longer and the last one left me with one long, rattling sigh. My father sat me upright next to him, his arm around my shoulders.

He was smiling.

"Tell me . . . how," I managed.

He talked then, because he was able to and I wasn't, and explained how he had been told that it was his turn to go to the site of the last shelling and scavenge the corpses of the Americans. *Ordered* to scavenge, he said bitterly. "Like hyenas. That's what we are to them."

By then, he told me, the fighting was so intense, he knew there was no way he was going to make it back to Casalvieri alive. "All I could think about was being brought back into the village dead in the back of that filthy, bloody truck."

After he had been ordered to scavenge the bodies, he came up with a very simple plan. After making it to the battlefield, strewn with dead bodies, he and the man sent out in the German vehicle with him found fresh corpses that had not yet progressed to rigor mortis.

"They let you drive alone?" I broke in. "Why didn't you drive away?"

He shook his head. "There was nowhere to drive. There is only the one road coming down from the gap, and the Germans controlled it. We had another, awful plan, and it involved those recent dead that we discovered.

"The whole time, I was convinced a sniper was going to put a bullet in my head. I kept ducking down at the slightest sound and I probably took twice as long because of it."

They switched clothing and scrounged up hand grenades to put with the German landmine they had stolen before leaving that morning.

"All we had to do then," Papa explained, "was hide among the bodies at a safe distance, throw the grenades at the truck, and listen to the explosion."

During the telling of the story, several candles were lit, throwing light on the interior, making my father's face look dark and haggard.

"It was gruesome, but effective. When the Germans came to investigate, body parts were everywhere, and even if they hadn't discovered our clothing on some of the pieces, the explosion would have been enough to convince them we couldn't possibly have survived. So then we were able to escape into the woods and circle back."

He took a drink from a small cup of wine.

"We had been able to keep in touch with the other men from the village," he continued. "That's how we knew about this place and how to get here, but it was still awful, finding our way back, waiting to run into the Germans, who would have been more than happy to execute us on the spot."

He stood and paced in front of me, the nervous energy coming back to him from the experience.

"The biggest fear we had, though, was that we would stumble across American soldiers, very much alive American soldiers, and they would see us in their fallen comrades' uniforms. They would not have treated us kindly."

I shuddered at the thought.

"As soon as I could, I tried to send word to you that I was all right, but communication with the village can be a risky thing, Benedetta. There are dangers. The Germans know men are in the mountains, but for now they leave us alone; they have bigger fish to fry. We must be careful not to draw their attention."

"How did you send word to Zizi Checcone, Papa? And why did you send for me?"

Papa smiled. "We got word to Signora Checcone several days ago . . ."

"Several days!" I was shocked. "She didn't say a word to me!"

"She's a smart woman, Benedetta. She was worried your emotions might give you away, so she waited and told you only what you needed to know."

I couldn't help but laugh; she had been right to do it. I filed away the feeling I had that Papa's voice had warmed dramatically at the mention of Zizi Checcone.

"And Dominic brought you here all right?"

"Dominic?" I asked.

But Papa was looking toward the door, through which walked a young man. He looked thin and gawky, his face pale. Surely, there was a mistake, I thought. This could not be the man who brought me up the mountain.

"Dominic Giancarlo," my father said, gesturing toward the young man. "From Roselli." Roselli was a village even smaller than Casalvieri, about fifteen or twenty miles to the north.

"It is nice to meet you properly, Benedetta," he said, shaking my hand, and I looked into those eyes, those eyes that were forever burned into my memory, and I knew that yes, this was the man, the boy, who had brought me up the mountain.

His dark pants were in tatters, and his shirt was much too small for him, his hands and wrists jutting out from his sleeves. His face was classically lean, his forehead full, and I thought back to the poster on Lauretta Fandella's wall. Yes, he was much better looking than Enrico Caruso.

Right then, I made a vow never to introduce him to Lauretta.

He took my hand.

"I did not hurt you, did I?" he asked, his voice deep and rough, completely at odds with the gentleness of his manner. The movement of speaking transformed his lean, angular face, softened it somehow and revealed the white teeth behind narrow, sensuous lips. And those eyes.

I looked at Papa, caught the curious expression on his face as he noted that Dominic had still not released my hand.

"Hurt?" Papa asked.

"I'm fine," I answered.

"We ran into a German on the path. I knocked him out and we ran. But in the process, it got a little rough getting Benedetta out of there."

It seemed then that Papa saw the scratches on my face, but the sleeves of my sweater hid the bruises.

"Dear Jesus," he said, crossing himself.

"Papa, I'm fine. Dominic took good care of me."

"Thank you, Dominic. Thank you," Papa said. He got off the cot and embraced Dominic. "I knew I was right to send you. You are the best of us on the mountain. I knew you could handle anything."

Dominic nodded. "It was my pleasure, Alfredo." He smiled at me and there was a twinkle in his eye. "It's not every day that a beautiful girl throws up on me."

I burst out laughing and my father looked from me to Dominic and then back to me. He didn't know what we were talking about but joined in the laughter anyway.

My eyes went back to Dominic. I wondered if at that moment he could tell that, high on a mountain in an ancient stone cabin surrounded by war and death, I had just reached one of the most important milestones in my life.

I was in love.

CHAPTER EIGHTEEN

—

In the very early morning, when it was still dark outside, the men inside the small cabin began to stir. A pot of coffee brewed over the small, crude fireplace. A man in a torn flannel shirt and thick, striped pants quietly shuffled cards at the lone table in the center of the room; he proceeded to lay the cards out on the tabletop for a game of solitaire.

I sat up and the pain in my back shot through me; these cots were awful. Even as tired as I was from the walk up the mountain, getting to sleep had been a major effort. Next to me, Papa swung his feet off his own cot and stood slowly. He put his hands in the small of his back like I had seen him do thousands of times, and stretched, letting out a low, deep groan. He caught my eye and smiled. There wasn't a lot of talking done last night; after Papa had told me about his escape, the shock of the trip up the mountain had worn off and I had at last fallen asleep.

"Now it is your turn to talk, Benedetta." Papa's eyes, full of concern, looked into mine. "How are you? How are the Germans treating you?"

I hesitated and my father placed a finger under my chin and raised my face, forcing me to look him in the eye. Images of Wolff, Schlemmer, and even the bishop flashed through my head, but I answered quickly.

"As to be expected. I cook. I clean. I do what they ask. They do not bother me."

"Good. Good. Do not be frightened. I have eyes in the village who are helping. You are not alone. How are Iole and Emidio?"

"They miss you, but we keep them busy, and I try to make up for you being gone, but I don't know how much that helps. In some ways, it is good that they are young; there will still be much time for them to recover."

His look was not the reaction I had hoped for; he seemed saddened by the thought of Iole and Emidio. "War changes everything, doesn't it, Benny?"

"Will things ever be the same? Will they ever go back to normal, Papa?"

He considered the question for a moment.

"I don't think so," he said. "I don't think so."

He shook his head sadly and then looked around the cabin. "Let me introduce you to the men."

I recognized some of the faces of men from Casalvieri.

Father led me to a man with a dark beard and a dark red hat. He wore thick black glasses and was in the process of cleaning the lenses.

"Benny, this is Vincenzo Benucci. He is from Roselli."

We shook hands.

"Nice to meet you, Benedetta. I've heard a lot about you from this *scarpencia*," he said, gesturing to my father. In our dialect, *scarpencia* means a parent who is too proud, going on and on about his children. In this instance, though, it wasn't meant to be insulting. It was a compliment to me.

"Alfredo," Benucci said. "You have a beautiful daughter."

"Thank you, Vincenzo. She's just like her mother." I looked at the floor, embarrassed for many reasons.

"How are things in Casalvieri, Benedetta?"

"Food is in short supply, but we are surviving. The German supplies, when they come in, are good, but they are not coming in very often anymore. Not like at the beginning."

"They are being stretched too thin," Papa said.

"Everyone thinks the Germans are beginning to lose their enthusiasm for fighting," I said. "They are not as proud as when they first arrived. They look tired."

"They may be losing this war," Benucci replied. "But they will never lose their will to fight. It is why the Germans were put on this earth. They are a stubborn, arrogant people, bred to conquer or to die trying. They will never change; they will never give up until they are dead or control the entire world."

"They are not like Italians," Papa said. "The Germans are cold and metallic as their armored tanks; their only passion is war."

"And us?" Signor Benucci asked my father.

"We are passionate about everything but war. Food. Wine. Art. Music. We are alive!"

"Don't forget cards," the man from the table said, slapping down another card to the sound of laughter in the room.

Papa and I continued to make our way around the room. Many of the faces were familiar, men from Casalvieri who asked about their families. I was able to tell them what I knew, which wasn't a whole lot.

Breakfast was a thick slice of stale bread and one more cup of coffee. Faint shafts of sunlight began to filter into the room and one by one, the men started to leave.

"Where does everyone go?"

"We try to get some of our work done, but we also all have our own places," Papa replied. "It is good not to know where everyone is, just in case."

Just in case the Germans find one of the men and torture him into telling about the others, I thought to myself.

"Even though we don't have to be too concerned about the Germans up here, it is better to be safe," Papa said. "An old man was shot last week near Montattico, just a few hours' walk from here."

"So is it safe here or not?"

"It is not safe anywhere in Italy."

"Do the Germans know about this place?"

Papa shrugged.

"It is safe to assume they do, but they would waste a lot of time and effort coming up here. Still, it is better not to gamble; that's why we leave during the day and go deeper into the woods. The Germans do not come out at night; they are scared of the *ribelli*."

"The men here . . ." I started to ask.

Papa shook his head.

"We are not part of the Resistance. There have been many talks, many arguments in this very room about this matter. Some of the younger men want to fight, to sabotage, but the older men like me fear too much for their families."

He washed down the last hunk of bread with his coffee. The look on his face betrayed his dislike for the flavor.

"If we were to raid a German supply convoy and men from Casalvieri, even one man from Casalvieri, were captured—ten people in the village would be executed. Colonel Wolff told as much to me. I believe him."

Papa looked into his empty coffee cup.

"The men here, we are ashamed."

"Papa . . ." I started to object.

"It's true, Benedetta. We are ashamed. We are men. We all, young and old alike, want to fight the *Germanesi*. I love my country as much as the Americans love theirs. But they don't have Germans in their homes, with guns pointing at their families."

He tried to pour any remaining coffee from the pot, but dregs plopped out into his cup.

"It may be dishonorable, but blowing up a German truck is not worth the price of my family, or anyone else's family in Casalvieri."

I went to him and sat on his lap, throwing my arms around him.

"It is your duty to be a father, to make it through this war in one piece," I said. "Fight to stay alive, Papa. That is the battle you need to win."

He kissed my forehead.

"Are you ready to go?" he asked, pulling on his boots.

"Where to?"

"I'll show you."

CHAPTER NINETEEN

—

Y ou will spend the day with us and the night, and then very
early tomorrow morning, you will return to Casalvieri," my
father said.

I hugged him for the fiftieth time.

"I am so happy I don't have to go back right away," I said. "Zizi
Checcone said Wolff would be gone for several days."

"But we don't want to take any chances," Papa said. "One day
we will spend together, and then you must go back."

"Are we going to hide?" I asked.

"We are going to scatter, but we will get some work done, too,"
Papa answered.

The men of Italy who had scattered to the mountains had little
to do there, save for one important thing: staying alive. Most of the
men were simply hiding, but some were rumored to have formed
themselves into guerrilla bands known as *ribelli*. Some of the *ribelli*
were politically motivated; they received some payment from their
organization's political party affiliations. In additional to a small
monthly stipend, they received food and clothing, news of their

home and families, all routed to them through a complex chain of communications. Mostly, the women and children of the villages carried messages hidden beneath their hats, in their shoes, even tucked underneath babies in carriages. It was an extensive support network structured to keep the partisans alive in order to disrupt the German military machine while also keeping any support well hidden from spies.

For men like Papa, however, who did not belong to a partisan political unit, survival was a much more rigorous job, as he explained when we set out from the cabin that morning.

"The few people who live here are friendly to us, and help us when they can. They won't hide us, though. For that, they would either be killed, sent to the front, or sent back to Germany."

"Sent back to Germany?" I asked. "For what?"

"Slave labor. I heard the Germans at the front talking about it. There are many dangerous jobs in the munitions plants in Germany, factories that make things for the war," he said. "Apparently, they have killed too many Jews, and now need Italian slaves to do the work. Naturally, the jobs are the most dangerous they can find, and workers usually only last a year or two. That's why there is such a demand."

Every day it seemed to get worse. I thought of families being torn apart, couldn't imagine what it would be like to be sent to Germany to work and probably die in one of their factories. It seemed to me that just because the Germans didn't kill you didn't mean that your life wasn't going to end.

I thought about that fact as Papa, Dominic, and I walked deeper into the woods at daybreak, heading due east through thick brush and fallen trees where there was no trail. We picked our way carefully, trying to avoid any kind of poison ivy and the worst of the brush that could slice open skin.

After almost an hour of walking, we came to a particularly dense patch of forest with many freshly fallen trees, probably knocked down by either a bomb or a bad storm. The area was so thick with trees and brush, there was little concern about German soldiers.

Papa quickly selected a tree and he and Dominic set to work. With ancient axes, they chopped the thick branches off from the main trunk, reducing them to pieces of firewood perfect for a country fireplace. I stacked the pieces in neat pyramids.

Dominic did most of the chopping, his young but wiry arms swinging the ax with precision and surprising force. Soon, there was more than enough wood to carry. In fact, we left many pyramids to perhaps retrieve later.

While Dominic chopped, my father had fashioned crude packs of burlap, each of us carrying as much wood as we could manage, considering the hike would take a fair amount of time.

We walked upward then, higher on the mountain and at a cross-cut angle from the direction in which we had come. Finally, after many rests for my father, who was huffing and puffing far worse than me, we arrived at a crude farmhouse. Dominic, who had barely broken a sweat on the hike even though he had by far the heaviest pack, approached the front door. There was no answer to Dominic's knock, and we discussed the possibility of the farmhouse being abandoned, but soon an old man came around from the back and gestured with a hand that we should follow him, which we promptly did.

We went around the house and unloaded the wood on a pile of firewood that looked like it too had been chopped recently. This had obviously been done before for the same reason we were doing it. Papa had said he personally had never brought wood for this farmer, but that the farm's location had no doubt made the list of other groups hiding in the area as a place that was friendly toward the mountain hideaways.

The old man was short and stooped, his shirt collar buttoned all the way to the top button, and he had a crude pipe from which curled tobacco smoke.

Almost on cue, when the last piece of wood hit the pile, an old woman, looking eerily similar to the old man, except without the pipe, opened the back door of the house. She had a small bag in her hands, which she handed to Papa.

"Grazie," said Papa.

"I wish we had more to give but we're running low, too," the old man said with a shrug.

"It is more than enough," Papa said, even though he hadn't looked inside the bundle yet. When he handed it to me, I didn't look inside either.

"Do you have any news?" Papa said.

The old man looked at us and I noticed that one of his eyes was milky white. His other eye focused on us clearly.

"Some planes flew by several days ago and they dropped parachutes. I think there were many dropped, but it looked like one was late getting out of the plane. It landed somewhere over there," he said, pointing a gnarled finger in the general direction of a meadow surrounded by steep, rocky hills. The hand shook slightly in the air.

"I would have gone and looked for it, but it is too far, and these aren't what they used to be," he said, gently slapping his knees.

Papa and Dominic exchanged looks. They seemed to have reached a decision, because Papa spoke.

"Did you tell anyone else about the parachute?" he said gently.

The old man shook his head.

"Do you know what color the parachute was?"

"I think it was yellow," the old man answered. "But this one is completely useless," he said, pointing to the cloudy eye. Then he pointed to the other one. "And this isn't much better."

"Enough of this talk!" the old woman said. "You sound like an old mule waiting to die! Should I put you out in the pasture?"

"You don't make it any easier, woman!" the old man retorted. "If I can survive your cooking this long, I've cheated death for too long already!"

He shot a wink at us.

"Well, we don't have time to go off chasing parachutes," said Papa. "Thanks for the supplies, though."

The old man reached out with a gnarled hand and shook Dominic's and Papa's hands. Then he and the woman retreated inside the house, muttering to each other.

Once we were out of earshot of the house, Papa turned to Dominic and me. He was smiling.

"This is too good an opportunity to pass up, no?"

We both nodded in agreement.

CHAPTER TWENTY

—

Once out of sight of the farmer's house, we circled around and paused briefly to decide the best strategy to find the parachute. We determined Papa would search the area nearby, as he could not move as quickly as we could, while Dominic and I covered the terrain along the far edge of the meadow along the base of the steep hills.

I walked with Dominic because I wanted to. After chasing him up the mountain the night before, I knew I could keep up with him. Besides, there was a bit of a thrill to the chase, and a part of me wanted to be the one who found the parachute and all the surprises that might be inside.

As soon as Dominic and I started walking, I asked him about the color of the parachute and why it was important enough for Papa to ask the old man about it.

"The Americans use different-colored parachutes to identify what kind of cargo is inside. I don't know all the different colors and what they mean, but I do know a few," he said. "Black is the most important and the most dangerous."

"Dangerous?"

"Black parachutes, from what I've heard—I've never actually found one—supposedly have radio equipment and disassembled weapons. Rifles, pistols, machine guns, hand grenades."

"They're dangerous because they might explode upon landing?"

He laughed.

"No, no. Because if the Germans catch you with either a radio or a gun, they will execute you immediately. Especially the radio. They hate radios. Many Germans have been killed because of *ribelli* radioing their locations to the Allies, so they take revenge upon anyone they find with a radio." His blue eyes blazed in the shade of the trees. "And if they find you with either one, radio or gun, it is not just you they will go after. Friends, family, children. No one is immune."

"They assume you're spying . . ."

He nodded. "Just for having those things in your possession."

Suddenly, I wasn't so eager to find the parachute.

"Red parachutes usually have medical supplies," Dominic continued.

"And yellow?" I asked.

"The best one of all for us: food. Coffee, sugar, flour, cigarettes, and even chocolate."

"That's why we're going to try to find this one?"

"That's why."

We scrambled over a large rock pile choked with weeds, possibly the remnants of a misguided bomb. I was once again amazed by the devastation the war was having on the land itself. Like the people who inhabited it, nothing was left untouched.

As we picked our way through thick brush and the occasional rocky outcroppings, I was struck even more by the easy grace of Dominic Giancarlo. His long body moved fluidly, never seeming to bring down all of his weight on his feet, constantly springing from one step to the next. Supple strength and a mind accustomed to walking in the mountains gave him that ability.

When the going was easy, we walked side by side. When the rough path we were following narrowed, Dominic would lead the way. If we had to climb over a steep bank, he would climb over, then reach back and pull me up, his big hands wrapped around my forearm, his fingers like iron on my skin.

We talked as we walked, mostly about him, because he seemed to know a lot about me already, having spent time with my father.

Dominic told me about Roselli, about where he lived, and that he was the third child, with two older brothers. They, too, were in the mountains, he said, but were staying with a different group for the time being.

"Do the men in the mountains move around much?" I asked.

"Yes. I have been with my brothers at their hideout, and they have been with us. Our plan was to spread out and see where the best place to hide from the Germans would be, but the truth is, they're pretty much all the same. Isolated areas of farmland where there is very little food and water, rough conditions, but, thankfully, few Germans. That last bit is the most important part."

Dominic related to me the story of how he had managed, along with his brothers, to escape to the mountains immediately upon the Germans' arrival. A young couple from Roselli had been on the outskirts of town late at night and heard the sound of the German vehicles approaching.

"What were they doing, the young couple?"

Dominic looked at me strangely, then raised an eyebrow.

"Oh," I said, blushing.

He said that they had been able to warn the people of Roselli, an even smaller town than Casalvieri, that the Germans were arriving, and the message spread like wildfire.

"My mother woke us up." Dominic smiled, remembering. "She was practically screaming at us to run. She scared the hell out of us." He laughed, rolling his eyes. "My brother Antonio took forever to wake up. Momma practically broke off one of his toes trying to get him awake. He snores so loud it's ridiculous. I think the men hiding with him in the mountains are ready to turn him over to the Germans."

Now it was my turn to laugh.

"Anyway," he said, "Momma threw some extra clothes at us and gave us all the bread in the house and sent us on our way."

"She didn't want to take any chances with her sons."

He nodded. "Some of the other younger men in the village didn't make it. They got caught on their way out, and went to the front two days later. Most of them are dead now."

"Is your father in the mountains too?" I asked, realizing that he had not mentioned his father at all yet. Normally I wouldn't have brought it up, but I wanted to know everything about this young man.

At the sound of the word *father*, Dominic's stride hesitated. He stopped and looked me in the eye, then, as if coming to a decision, he answered.

"My father disappeared many years ago. From what people told Momma, he was just an unhappy man. Didn't want to work the land, and so he did what he wanted—he left."

"I'm sorry, Dominic, I didn't mean to . . ."

He waved a hand.

"No, it's all right. We did fine without him. From what Momma said, he wasn't much help anyway."

We walked on for quite a while in silence. Up ahead, a peak loomed larger as we approached. It was our compass point. The old man said that we should walk straight toward it. It was difficult to see too far ahead because the land rose and dipped so frequently. We couldn't get a real glimpse of what lay ahead until we topped the jagged and unpredictable hills.

We climbed a constantly shifting hill of soft clay, small rocks, and thick stands of juniper bushes. Dominic went over the top first and when I followed him, reaching the bottom, I crashed into his back. We both went down in a heap and when we stood up, there was the parachute on the ground, wrapped in its thick fabric.

There were animal tracks around it, but for the most part nothing seemed disturbed. The depression in which the parachute lay was guarded on both sides by the steep banks, and the thick grass, along with shadow, made the bright yellow less visible. It was easy to understand why it had gone unnoticed for this amount of time.

From the way the parachute sat on the ground, it looked like the cylindrical metal tube containing the cargo had cracked on a rock and shattered into many pieces. Boxes were strewn around the small depression. Several had split open, and one had spilled cartons of American cigarettes onto the ground.

Dominic turned to me.

"I'll start bundling these things together. Go back and get your father. Hurry. The German lookouts keep an eye out for these, and they will have sent a search party. We have to assume we don't have much time."

CHAPTER TWENTY-ONE

—

I topped out on the first rise, the one Dominic and I had fallen down together, and looked back toward where we had left Papa. I felt a small surge of fear; I hadn't paid close enough attention to where we were going when I walked with Dominic. I was too busy thinking about him, about his hands, and lips. *Stop!* I told myself. It was time to concentrate, to find Papa, get the goods from the parachute, and then get to the cabin.

Working my way back, I hurried, hoping to find him and get back as soon as possible. I had never seen anything like the cargo inside the parachute! All that food! There was enough flour in that barrel to feed a family for a year. Not to mention the goodies: the coffee, the cigarettes, and the chocolate! Oh! I felt like telling Dominic and Papa to keep everything, but give me the chocolate.

Soon, it was necessary to slow down. I realized that, in addition to not paying enough attention while walking to the parachute, I was now walking the same path but this time going in the opposite direction, which changed everything. All the landmarks were different. The rock piles looked different; the trees stood out at opposite angles. And when I looked back, even that didn't help.

With each hill, I stood and scanned the land before me. But with many rises and depressions in the field, Papa could easily remain hidden. He had said he would search nearby then rest and wait, but that if he had the strength, he would follow our line and meet us coming back. Now I was starting to have my doubts. The fear that had been seeping into my stomach now started bubbling, like a pot of water heating to a boil.

Finally, I began waving my arms at each of these higher out-croppings and at last, I received an answering wave, slightly off to the right of where I was headed. Was he off course or was I?

Carefully marking my spot with a small pile of sticks, I raced toward the waving arms. I knew Papa would be so happy and so proud. There would be a celebration at the cabin tonight; that was certain. And it was something Dominic and I had found together. There was something I liked about the sound of "together" being used in the same breath as Dominic's name and mine.

My feet flew over the rocky ground, hurtling me closer to my father. As I ran, I could hear the sound of voices.

I stopped in my tracks.

The voice I heard was speaking German.

The fear gripped me and I stopped breathing. I heard another voice hush the first one. They were waiting for me and they knew I was close.

I stood riveted to the ground. I had no weapon. No radio. I was a young girl; surely they would not think I was a spy. The questions would certainly come, though. Who was I? Where was my family? What was I doing here?

And were the Germans searching for the parachutes? Or were they the soldiers I'd heard about, who were hunting the *ribelli*?

I had to do something. If I ran and they caught me, they might kill me. Better to just turn myself in, show that they were not my enemies, and that I wasn't theirs. They would understand, certainly.

I started forward, but then the image of Schlemmer's face filled my mind's eye—his yellow teeth, his mad-dog eyes—and I dropped to the ground and began to half crawl, half crab walk backward. Because of the uneven terrain, I was able to negotiate my way around the hills, taking care not to silhouette myself against the sky.

Soon, breathless, I was back to my pile of sticks. With a strength driven by fear, I raced back to the parachute, not sure of what I would find there, and not sure if the Germans would be following me.

I stumbled several times, scraping both knees and twisting an ankle. Blood from my knees streamed down my shins, but I felt no pain. My hair was sweaty and tangled; it stuck to my face and strands were in my mouth. My chest heaved; my legs burned.

I must have looked like a crazy woman when I stumbled over the last hill, slid down the bank, and landed almost right on top of my father.

"Benny!" he said, catching me in his arms. "I just got here! I was panicking!"

I was completely out of breath, and turned to face the direction from which I had come.

I pointed, but no sound came.

Hurriedly, Dominic and Papa hoisted the bags they had made from torn sections of the parachute onto their shoulders. The makeshift bags were bulging with supplies.

"What, Benny?" my father asked.

"Germans," I finally got out.

"*Brutta bestia,*" my father said, scooping me into his arms. "Come," he said to Dominic.

We ran from the parachute, my father taking the lead, me in the middle, and Dominic bringing up the rear. I concentrated on putting one foot in front of the other, trying to block the pain coming from my legs. I gulped air when Papa stopped to get his bearings or conferred with Dominic on the best way to go.

We raced in the opposite direction from the Germans, then gradually circled back and headed for the safety of the woods. When I heard my father's breathing start to labor, I ran alongside him. Finally, I lifted the pack from his shoulder and ran ahead. He seemed to want to protest, but couldn't manage to produce the oxygen required.

When we reached the woods' edge, we stood together and looked back. We felt safe, at least for the time being.

CHAPTER TWENTY-TWO

—

The crude fireplace held a small fire—small because, although it needed to generate enough heat to cook the food, it also needed to create as little smoke as possible. A screen made of wire mesh and sticks was placed over the top of the chimney to break up what little smoke did escape.

A pot over the fire held bubbling tomato sauce, a creation that drew much attention from the men assembled in the small room.

The bread had been baked, not in an oven but in the back corner of the fireplace. It wasn't scientific, but it was the area of the hearth that most likely enjoyed the most consistent temperatures. From time to time, I turned the bread so it would bake evenly. The loaves were thick and rich. It was solid bread, the kind no one in the cabin, myself included, had seen in a long time. It drew *ooh*s and *aah*s when I slid the first loaves out of the hearth.

By the time the men returned in the evening from their hiding places, Dominic, Papa, and I had the treasure spread out on top of the big table. The haul from the fallen parachute was impressive. Even after the goods had been split up among the men to be distributed to their families in the villages, there was enough left over to last the cabin's inhabitants for several months, as well as to make a celebration dinner, the job of which had fallen gladly onto my shoulders.

After the men feasted their eyes on the goods, and as the first aroma of my cooking began to make its way through the tiny cabin, the men responded appropriately. From out of shirt pockets and packs came a few ingredients, not enough, but at least something. A small clove of garlic, part of an onion, a rolled-up cloth that inside held a pocket of rich black pepper. One of the men had trapped and killed a fresh rabbit. The tender meat was added to the sauce along with the ingredients. Although not enough for a strong, bursting flavor, the meat and spices would be the delicacy, the hinting of familiar tastes that the men would enjoy.

A bottle of wine hidden for many months was brought out, along with nuts and a small brick of cheese that had managed to elude mold. The cards were placed on the table, shuffled, and immediately a card game began. An older man pulled out an accordion and proceeded to inspire several men to dance before the fireplace, toasted by their comrades.

Dominic watched all with a frequent smile, but he seemed somewhat quiet, observing the activities. Several times, I caught him looking at me, whereupon he quickly turned away, pretending not to notice. The cooking duties kept me busy, and I also pretended not to notice his looks.

Even after I knew the sauce was ready, I let it simmer longer than necessary, to draw out the occasion and let the men enjoy themselves a little bit longer. The accordion played on, the cards kept hitting the table, and the wine was still flowing.

Finally, the accordion player put down his instrument and looked at me questioningly.

"Bring your plates," I called.

The men reached quickly for their battered metal plates and forks.

"Ah, Heaven awaits," the first man in line said. I ladled a mound of pasta onto his plate, then smothered it with the thick sauce, being sure to include a hunk of meat. There would probably be just enough for each man to have a piece. Next to the pasta I put a thick slice of bread on his plate.

"*Grazie, Signora,*" he said.

All the men filed through, except for Dominic and my father. Dominic approached first.

"It feels good to cook food you caught yourself, no?" he said, grinning.

I laughed and checked the bottom of the pot. There were several pieces of meat left, so I ladled a few extra onto Dominic's plate along with the rich red sauce.

"*Grazie,* Benedetta," he said. Breathing the sauce's aroma deeply, he said, "It takes beauty to create beauty."

I blushed and looked away, muttering a thank-you.

My father stepped up as Dominic turned and Papa caught my expression, but his eyes revealed nothing.

I scraped all of the meat together, many pieces, and ladled them onto my father's plate. He started to object but I cut him off. "Hush," I said. "You need strength, Papa. Strength to come home." I emphasized the last word and he closed his mouth.

The cabin had gone from loud and boisterous to eerily silent as the men dug into their meals, savoring the rich sauce and hearty bread. It was a meal they remembered from a long time ago, back when they were with their families. Back before the Germans came.

I sat next to Papa and we ate in silence. He looked at me and shook his head in wonder at the meal.

"You are a magician, little girl," he said.

One by one, the men finished their meals, put their plates down, and leaned back, some with their hands clasped across their bellies, others stretched out on their makeshift mattresses. When the last one put down his plate, they turned as one to me and started clapping.

"*Bravissimo!*" some of them called out.

A small bottle of anisette was passed around and poured into the metal cups. A bowl of nuts and wild berries followed. It wasn't much for dessert, but enough to put a sweet taste in the mouth and take the edge off the heavy aftertaste of the sauce and bread.

After the men cleaned their plates (most of the sauce had been wiped clean already with bread) the card game quickly resumed and the accordion player picked up his instrument once again. But instead of the lively tune he had been belting out, this was a slow song, full of emotion and gentle cadence. Some of the men seemed to be sad; the aftermath of the festive feeling was one of wistfulness for family to be near.

A heavy, thickset man approached and asked if he could have the honor of cleaning the big black pot used to cook the sauce. I nodded and he produced a thick piece of bread and proceeded to wipe the sides of the pot with slow, deliberate strokes. Each stroke produced an oily, rich spread. The man ate with slow ecstasy, winking at me once in the process.

Dominic slowly made his way across the room and stood before Papa and me.

"Signor Carlesimo, would I offend you by asking your daughter if she would like to accompany me on a walk?"

Papa smiled, but remained silent. I would realize much later what that hesitation meant.

"Benny, do you want to go for a walk with Dom?"

I was trying desperately not to blush, feeling the eyes of my father as well as the other men in the cabin upon me.

"It is a nice night for a walk," I said.

"Go. But be careful. Not too far." He looked back down at the walnuts in his hand, popping more into his mouth, followed by a drink of wine.

I stood and followed Dominic out the door.

CHAPTER TWENTY-THREE

———

Night breezes stirred the broad leaves of the trees as Dominic and I left the cabin. Crickets sang their songs, unaware that their audience had grown by two. The crisp light of the stars illuminated the night and, complemented by the phosphorescence of the half-moon, made the ground seem to glow.

Once again, I felt the clumsiness I first experienced on the walk up the mountain. Dominic's feet seemed to glide over the soft grass and occasional lump of fallen leaves. He made no sound while I clumped along, stumbling a bit, stepping normally only to find a rise of rock that jarred my leg from my ankle to my knee all the way up to my hip and lower back. I hoped Dominic didn't see every misstep, but I think he did. His eyes seemed to miss nothing. Even in the dark.

Tomorrow, I would go down the mountain, but tonight there was love in my heart.

I felt torn about going back. I knew that Iole and Emidio needed me. Zizi Checcone would take good care of them; there was no doubt in my mind about that. But they hadn't been away from Papa or me for this long ever before. I knew they would be scared and wondering where we were.

But I wanted to stay with Papa. As ridiculous as it sounded, I felt like I could protect him. The very thought of anyone trying to hurt Papa made my blood boil. I wanted to tear Colonel Wolff apart with my bare hands for sending Papa to the front. The *Germanesi* would pay one day for this.

We walked across the small meadow to an opening in the forest. A path wound its way up the side of a steep rise, and on the right side we could look down into a shallow valley. Even with the light of the moon, the trees below shielded the ground and left much of the land in the dark. It was a winding trail that took us through thick forest and then out into a brief patch of more mountain meadow. Water was close; I once heard the sound of a fish splashing.

At first, our conversation was awkward. Although we had been alone together on our first walk up the mountain, that had seemed more like business. And the walk to the parachute had seemed like a mission, a task at hand. But this walk—there was no doubt about this walk. This was about pleasure. Just the two of us. My hands were clammy and my heart felt light in my chest. Every few moments it would flutter and I would fight it down, tell myself to relax and be calm. We talked about many things, and the more we walked, the more fluid the conversation became, and I opened up to Dominic, something I was never very good at with friends and even family. I told him some of my hopes and dreams, and he told me some of his.

Without speaking, our hands came together and we walked slowly, breathing in the crisp night air.

There was something about him, his ease, that made me feel comfortable. He felt like a member of my family already, someone I could speak with and trust. This was not a feat easily accomplished, as my mother's philosophy had always been to trust no one—"not even Jesus on the cross," she had told me once, which had shocked me.

The way Dominic held himself—his natural humor, his gentle way—made me think of Emidio. This was always how I imagined Emidio would be when he got older.

"Your father is a good man," Dominic said. "I respect him very much."

"He has been through a lot."

"He depends on you."

"Who else does he have?"

He looked at me carefully. "I know your mother passed away . . ." he said.

I thought of our conversation on the way to the parachute, in which Dominic talked about his father leaving the family.

So I told him.

I told him about my father coming back looking like a dead man, his eyes red with tears, trying to tell us what had happened, unable to find the words. The priest was with him, and we all prayed together. I didn't really understand what had happened, but I was old enough to know that my mother wasn't coming back. Iole and Emidio said that they understood, but for weeks after would ask Papa and me when Mama would be back and if she would have the new baby with her. Every time they asked, Papa would hide his face, the tears rolling down his cheeks. Finally I scolded them, tears in my own eyes. They stopped asking, eventually.

As I talked, the emotions just kept coming.

I told him about my mother. Her thick black hair always tied back in a bun. I told him about the arguments she and Papa would have, during which they were seemingly angry and about to kill each other, and then they would start laughing and dance around the room. Dominic listened as I told him about Mama's *vignio*, a branch selected from the tree out back. It was a wicked little branch she used when her children did something really bad. Like the time I said I was in love with Guido Angeluzzi, a boy who lived in the same village. Before I knew it, Mama had me across her lap, the *vignio* leaving white-hot burns across my buttocks.

I laughed, remembering it.

"She was the disciplinarian in our house," I said. "When Papa came home, he never scolded us; he was too glad to see us. So she told us she had to be the one who enforced the rules. And boy, did she ever."

"It sounds like she was a strong woman," Dominic said.

"Yes. But we all knew that she would tear off her own flesh to feed her children. She pinched pennies, but if we were ever sick, she bought the best medicine, she burned more oil and fed us the thick soup, even if it meant she would go hungry that night."

For a moment, I said nothing, transported back in time to when I had my mother. When I could be a little girl and she would make everything all right. She would take care of me. Now, it was different. Now, I did the taking care of.

"Are you thirsty?" Dominic asked.

"Yes," I said, realizing it was true. I had talked for a long time. And, surprisingly, I wasn't embarrassed. In fact, I felt peaceful.

"We should get back, too. But let's get a drink first," he said. "I know of a sweet creek up ahead that produces the coldest, purest water you'll ever taste."

We walked ahead, and this time Dominic stayed very close to me. I got the feeling he wanted to touch me, but it was not right. It was too soon, and although he didn't realize it, I wanted something much more from him.

Gradually, I began to hear the sound of gurgling water and we came to a rock formation cut into the side of a hill. In the moonlight, I could see the water glistening against the black rock, could see the wetness of the rock itself, but I saw no pool below.

Dominic stepped up the rock face and reached high. His hand disappeared over a rock shelf and then his hand came down, cupping a handful of ice-cold water. My parched throat and I watched with envy as he drank deeply.

He looked at me and we both realized with awkwardness that this could be a little tricky. I loved the idea of him putting his arms around me and lifting me up high, but somehow I didn't think Papa would approve. Especially considering that my dress was too small and if he lifted me too high, well, I didn't want him to see anything he shouldn't.

We looked around for some sort of crude cup, maybe a thick piece of bark I could shape into a drinking glass, but nothing presented itself.

"Scoop some for me," I said.

He looked at me strangely and then stretched once again. I heard his hand leave the water above, a gentle splashing sound.

Dominic brought his hand down and I guided it to my mouth. I held it close and drank deeply. He was right; it was delicious water, pure and cold.

I straightened up and he was looking at me as though shocked.

"You drank from my hand," he said. I saw something in his eyes I did not like.

Anger rose up inside me.

I grabbed his hand and opened it, for him to see. Then I held out my hand opened, next to his.

"Look. How is your hand different from mine?" I asked. He looked down. His hand was much bigger than mine, but we both had calluses, deep lines. Signs of hard work.

When he looked back up, his eyes were lowered, his face flushed.

"I saw the look in your eyes," I said, the anger coming in waves. "Who do you think you are, passing judgment on me? At a time like this, you worry what kind of girl I am?"

I turned on my heel and made my way back to the cabin. He didn't walk with me, but stayed behind, watching.

The next morning, I asked Papa to find someone else to take me down the mountain.

PART THREE

CHAPTER TWENTY-FOUR

Casalvieri at dawn. Sleepy stone walls reflected the soft orange glow of the early morning sun. I made my way through the narrow streets, feeling like I had been gone for years instead of days. Everything seemed smaller and distant, like an old photograph found in a new book.

I passed homes with no signs of life, no men leaving to work the fields, no children up to help with chores. There were no chores because there were no animals left. No crops to tend. Casalvieri itself was now a casualty of the war.

At my house, Zizi Checcone was busy in the kitchen, peeling vegetables and boiling water. I'd never met anyone who boiled as much water as Zizi Checcone.

"Benedetta," she cried softly, hugging me to her ample bosom. She put a finger to her lips and gestured with her chin toward the next room, then pulled me into the small pantry and leaned close with her lips against my ear.

"Wolff got back last night. He asked about you, but I said you weren't feeling well and were upstairs."

I nodded to let her know I understood.

We walked back to the kitchen and I started to help her with the vegetables.

"No," she said. "Go upstairs and wake up your brother and sister. They'll be happy to see you."

"Have they behaved?"

"Like angels. Now that you're back, I'm sure they'll start to act like little devils. They get more of your attention that way."

I laughed and ran up the stairs. I cracked the door, saw the lump of each of their bodies in their beds. Iole was on her side, her mouth open, drool on the pillow. Emidio, as usual, was completely on top of his blanket, his head at the foot of the bed, his feet on his pillow. In his arms he clutched a worn teddy bear.

I felt a surge of pride, the kind that Papa must feel. I was their big sister, but had assumed the role of mother, and now I was feeling the emotions that a mother must feel.

I climbed onto Emidio's bed and he stirred slightly. I reached down and tickled the sole of his foot, which he immediately retracted under the pillow. He flopped his head on the other side and this time I grabbed his big toe, then slowly applied pressure. His eyes scrunched at the discomfort; he tried to pull his leg back but this time I was prepared and had a good grip.

"Ah!" he yelled, his eyes snapping open. I let go of his big toe and he looked at me, his eyes bleary, confused at first, and then he laid his head back down. I could see him focus, see the anger pool, then rise up in a wave.

"*Bestia!*" he yelled, and lunged at me. We nearly toppled off his bed, and, out of the corner of my eye, I saw Iole start to sit up, but then I was thrown down with surprising force onto Emidio's bed. He started to get a good grip on my hair, but then I flipped him over my shoulder and pounced on him, pinning him down with ease. I flicked his ears, something he could never tolerate.

"I hate that!" he said.

"Really?"

Flick. Flick.

Iole came bounding off her bed and jumped into my arms, her hug taking my breath away. I smelled her face and hair; the mustiness of the pillow and her morning breath mingled into the sweetest, most innocent smell in the world.

"I'm not done with her!" yelled Emidio, and he jumped over Iole, knocking her with his knees, and barreled into me with his square little head.

"Hey, you got me!" Iole snarled, and leapt on top of him. I followed, and pretty soon we were all giggling and laughing, squirming, and then we fell off the bed onto the floor.

"When did you get back?" Iole asked after we quieted down.

"This morning."

"Where were you? Drinking wine somewhere with the *ribelli,* I bet," Emidio said, a little smile on his face, inviting the attack, which he soon got.

"Get off of me!" he yelled.

"Your mouth is awfully fresh for a little boy," I said.

"You haven't heard the worst of it," Iole said with a sideways glance at her younger brother.

"He can't be any worse than you were," I said, rolling my eyes.

"I was not fresh!" Iole said.

"Ayee yah! You were awful!" I said. When she looked hurt, I tackled her and started tickling her tummy.

After I stopped, she looked at me.

"You sure are in a good mood. Did something nice happen to you while you were gone?"

I wanted to tell them. Wanted them to know that I had been led to believe Papa was dead and then found out he wasn't. I wanted them to realize how lucky they were, that they still had the greatest father in the world and that after we all got through this war alive and in one piece, the three of us would need to protect him, take care of him for as long as we could.

Instead I told them to get dressed, that playtime was over and it was time to get some work done.

"That's all you care about: work, work, work," Emidio complained as he pulled on his shirt and pants.

"Yeah, and you're lucky that's all I care about. Otherwise you'd be hungry with no clothes to wear, no warm bed to sleep in," I said. "I know other children who would trade places with you in a minute."

He looked embarrassed.

"And don't you ever forget it," I added unnecessarily.

As I watched him get dressed, a shadow fell over my shoulder and I turned, startled, to see Colonel Wolff in the doorway.

In the short time since I'd last seen him, he'd deteriorated rapidly. He looked like a man who was losing more than just a war.

"Benedetta," he said. His uniform was rumpled, his face was dirty, and he slouched. A far cry from the man who had sat ramrod straight in his chair that first morning the Germans arrived. "Come with me." He turned and started down the stairs, not waiting to see if I would follow.

"See if Zizi Checcone needs help," I said to Iole and Emidio.

And then I followed Wolff.

CHAPTER TWENTY-FIVE

———

Y ou Italians know nothing about drinking," he said, his words more than slurred. Wolff produced a bottle of schnapps and held it before me. His eyes were red and bleary, either from a lack of sleep or an abundance of alcohol. Or maybe both.

"Ah, now here, here is the nectar of the gods," he said. "Made in Germany! The Land of War Machines and the world's best schnapps!" He laughed.

Zizi had taken my brother and sister into a different room and now Wolff stood at the big table in the kitchen. He poured a dose of the schnapps into a large coffee cup, and then gestured with a lifting of his chin to the coffeepot on the hearth. I brought it to the table.

"Do you want me to heat it up?"

He shook his head and I poured the cold coffee into his cup, which was already half full with the clear liquor. The coffee thinned slightly, and pale clouds rose and swirled inside the light brown coffee as the two liquids mixed.

"If you think it is too early to drink, young Catholic girl," he said, "remember that I have been awake, fighting the forces of Allied

evil, for the last forty-eight hours. I intend to drink much of this"—
he brought his hand down on top of the bottle, the wedding band
on his finger clinking against the glass—"and when I have finished
consuming this gift from Heaven, I intend to sleep for at least a
day, maybe two. So you see, young Benedetta of the Mountains,
although it is, what, eight o'clock in the morning? This is really a
nightcap at this point."

"I understand, Colonel Wolff."

"Please, Hermann. And please, help yourself. I have been drinking alone far too long. They say that is the sign of an alcoholic."

"I intend to drink with you . . . Hermann," I said hesitantly.

"Good, good."

I put the coffeepot back on the stove and began to heat it, then
got a cup for myself from the cupboard. "However, while it is the
end of your day, it is merely the beginning of mine."

"You and I, Benedetta. We are like night and day, no?" he said,
convulsing into laughter at his joke.

The coffee would not be heated up enough, but I poured
myself a cup and was about to sit down when he spoke.

"Let's walk, Benedetta. It looks like a beautiful morning."

Zizi Checcone appeared in the doorway.

"You're going out, Benedetta? I need help with cleaning potatoes and making bread for today's meals." Her concern was poorly
concealed. I knew that the bread was already made and that a bucket
full of peeled potatoes sat just around the corner of the fireplace.

"Ah, woman," Wolff said, "there is hardly enough food for us
and you need help preparing it? I don't believe it. She will be all
right with me, Signora," he assured her.

Zizi Checcone looked like she was about to say something more
but then stopped. What was there she could do?

"Come, Benedetta. We walk and talk."

I followed him out into the bright morning light with my cup of lukewarm coffee. The sun had risen now and its warmth on my skin felt reassuring.

"Is there someplace we can sit and watch the day break in all its glory, capturing the beauty of this land for which so many men are dying?"

Whether it was a rhetorical question or not, I decided to answer. "If we walk this way, we will come to a small clearing where there are some crude benches overlooking the valley."

"That sounds perfect, Benedetta. Is it far? I am not up for a long walk." Already he was walking unsteadily, and as if on cue, he stumbled.

"Just a few minutes through those trees there," I said, pointing to a small knot of forest.

"Lead the way, Private Carlesimo."

We walked in silence, Wolff's breathing becoming labored as we trudged through the forest. When the path opened up onto the clearing, the view was truly gorgeous, with thick mist overhanging the valley, the tops of the trees poking through the clouds like plants bursting from the topsoil.

A lone, thick bench remained perched on the ledge overlooking the valley. We sat down together and Wolff refilled his cup, this time just straight schnapps.

"To a beautiful day," he said, raising his cup. I clinked it with mine.

"*Saluté.*"

He gulped his schnapps; I sipped my coffee.

"How's your father?" he said, and looked straight out into the valley, his face impassive.

My heart stopped. "What kind of horrible question is that?" I said, trying to strike the right chord of indignation.

Wolff looked at me out of the corner of his eye, then shrugged. "My apologies."

I thought I detected a smile behind the drunken eyes.

"It's just that there was some talk about the scene of the explosion; one of my men went to see if the vehicle was salvageable, which it wasn't," Wolff said. "He said some of the clothes found on the various body parts didn't seem to fit. I rejected it all as hearsay. Who knows what happens when a person gets blown apart, how it affects his clothing? No, your father definitely died in that explosion." He tossed off the rest of the schnapps in his cup and refilled it again.

"And we are three children with no parents," I said.

He patted my shoulder. "Ah, Benedetta, I've watched you. You are strong. Beautiful. Intelligent. You will raise your brother and sister. Find a good man to marry you. Your father's name will live on."

"The war is not over," I pointed out.

"But it soon will be."

I looked at him questioningly, but he didn't elaborate.

"I would be proud to call you my daughter," he said.

I felt my face flush.

He refilled his cup with more schnapps.

"But of course, that is pointless to consider, since you are not my daughter," he said. "And now that I have no wife, I will most likely never have a son or a daughter at all."

"You can marry again."

"And rebuild? A fresh start?" He laughed bitterly. "I have a feeling that when this war is over, everything will be destroyed. I see a future of rubble."

"Make what you can with the rubble," I said. "Is that not what life is?"

He laughed heartily. "You sound about as optimistic as Nietzsche. Did you know that he was a soldier?"

"Who is—?"

"He was a philosopher. A German. Our greatest German phi-losopher."

I shrugged.

"He is to Germany what Machiavelli is to Italy," Wolff said.

"Papa has one of his books. Machiavelli's, that is. *The Prince*, I think."

"Yes, yes. A great book. Ironic, isn't it, that your philosopher is famous for schemes to acquire power and conquer, while mine essentially despised the power of the state?"

"Under these conditions, I would have to say yes, it is ironic," I said. I wondered why Wolff wanted to talk about philosophers.

"And did you know that Machiavelli was a soldier?" he said.

"No, I didn't."

"Nietzsche was a soldier, too. He was in the army for a year. Nietzsche in artillery. Can you imagine that? Imagine during battle, praying to God, and having Nietzsche turn to you and say, 'God is dead. Now pick up that rifle and shoot someone!'"

He laughed again, and shook his head at the image.

"He wrote that 'madness is rare in individuals, but in groups, parties, nations, and ages, it is the rule.' Ah," Wolff said, "my applause, Friedrich. So prophetic."

"War is madness," I said, but he didn't seem to notice me, lost in his own thoughts and drunkenness.

"Nietzsche also wrote that 'under peaceful conditions, a war-like man sets upon himself.' That's simple, but I often wonder if the opposite is true: that under warlike conditions, a peaceful man sets upon himself. Do you agree?"

"I think some men are destined to set upon themselves, no mat-ter what the conditions," I said.

"Do you think I am one of those men?"

"No," I answered without hesitation. "Do you think you are?"

"Never before, but now . . ."

He spread his hands out before him, seeking an explanation. His hands shook.

"Now . . ." He drank the rest of his cup and then picked up the bottle and drank deeply from it, not bothering to pour some into the cup.

How long we sat there, I do not know. Wolff drank the rest of the schnapps, throwing the bottle from the edge of the cliff down into the valley. He sat back down and we looked at the view before us in silence.

He turned to me finally, about to say something, but instead slid off the bench, his knees hitting the dirt as his shoulders slumped. Tears streamed down his face; he collapsed against my legs and placed his head on my knee. Instinctively, I put my hand on top of his head and patted him, shocked at how old his face looked on my knee.

He fell asleep and stayed in the same position for an hour while I thought about dead philosophers and their thoughts on war. I was scared, too, wondering what I would do if German soldiers burst onto the scene and saw their leader kneeling before a young girl, as if in supplication, she petting his head like a stray dog.

Finally, Wolff awoke with a start.

His eyes struggled to adjust, and then he spoke. "How long?"

"About an hour and a half, maybe two."

He looked embarrassed as he stood and dusted off his uniform, then started off in the direction of the house. He wobbled slightly and I resisted the urge to help him.

We went the entire way back to the house in silence.

CHAPTER TWENTY-SIX

—

A week had passed since my trip to the mountain, and I had received no further word from my father. I prayed every night that he was doing well and that God was looking out for him.

When Wolff returned to the front, we had not discussed the scene on the bench overlooking the valley. Other than showing an incredible amount of pain and fatigue the next day from too much drinking, he didn't act as if anything noteworthy had happened between us. And I was more than happy to play along with it. If he was embarrassed, he did not let me see it, and I came to believe that in his mind it was simply a matter that had happened and was now over.

I wondered, though, if his return to the front had anything to do with what he had talked about. Was it to get into battle and fight, an attempt to reclaim his spirit for the war? Or was it perhaps to avoid another scene of drunkenness, sorrow, and anti-German sentiment? It was probably a lot harder to get falling-down drunk at the front. And a person's life must be in a whole lot of agony if running away to war is the better option.

My routine continued. Up early, build a fire in the fireplace, or if no wood was ready, chop enough to keep the stove going for the better part of the day. If bread needed to be baked and if flour was available, another fire would need to be built in the outdoor oven. Depending upon the amount of vegetables that were gathered, the process of scraping them together along with spices would be started, the end results always amounting to a very thin and very weak menestra.

Then laundry would need to be taken to the big pot outside, or to the springs. Cleaned, hung out to dry, then folded. If there was not any laundry, then the house would be cleaned—floors mopped, walls scrubbed, dust wiped away.

And then it would be time to start thinking of dinner. The search for a piece of meat to make a weak stew would begin. If we were lucky enough to find one, or a German soldier could produce a rabbit or squirrel, it would be thrown in with a few potatoes and any remaining onions from lunch.

Despite our efforts, everyone was getting too thin. The most dramatic change was in Zizi Checcone; she looked like a different woman, and the change was not altogether bad. I knew she wasn't eating much, and that she gave as much as she could to Iole and Emidio. I told her not to, that we needed her to keep strong, but she would pinch the dwindling roll of fat around her middle and say, "I've still got some reserves left. Who ever heard of a fat woman starving to death?"

On this morning, Zizi Checcone and I were in the kitchen, slicing bread and setting out plates and cups on the table, when Iole bounded in from outside, a thick, folded piece of paper in her hand.

"I've got a secret! I've got a secret!" she said, then laughed and danced around the big table. She waved the paper around and smiled, looking at me. Zizi Checcone and I ignored her and continued setting things out for dinner. Iole, however, refused to be ignored.

"So, Benedetta, who is Dominic Giancarlo?"

I whirled on her. "*Brutta bestia!*" I cried and chased her around the table, but she was fast—her long legs flashed and the paper was clasped tightly in her hand.

I stopped at one end of the table, and she at the other.

"Give me that, Iole. Right now."

"Dominic Giancarlo! Dominic Giancarlo!" Iole sang in her high voice, a big smile on her face.

I chased her around the table some more; I was laughing, but getting angrier at each circle around the table.

"Benedetta!" Zizi Checcone said sharply. "What is this all about?"

"Benedetta's got a boy!" Iole cackled and then she made a break for the stairs, but I chased her at an angle and caught her, then wrestled her to the ground and tore the paper from her hand.

"He's not my boy!" I stood, my face flushed.

Iole rolled and stood, then raced behind Zizi Checcone. "Judging by that letter, that's not what he thinks!"

I looked at the paper in my hand. My name was written clearly on the top fold.

"Do you always read letters addressed to someone else?" I walked toward her, hand held ready to slap her. *La mazatta.*

"Iole! Where are your manners? Your mother and father did a better job raising you than that!" The sharpness in Zizi Checcone's voice wiped the smile off Iole's face. She looked at the ground and I could see tears start to well up in her eyes.

"I'm sorry, Benedetta," my little sister said. The look on her face threw cold water on my anger.

"It's okay," I said, tousling her hair. "But I'll remember this when you're older." I smiled at her. She smiled back and wiped a tear from her eye.

"Where did you find it?" I asked.

"It was underneath a rock along the low stone wall by the barn." I nodded.

Zizi Checcone spoke. "Iole, help me with the potatoes. Benedetta, go read your letter." She threw a hand towel over Iole's shoulder and they both turned to the big pot over the fire as I ran upstairs to the bedroom, clutching the letter against my chest. I closed the door and lay on the bed, Emidio's teddy bear reading the letter over my shoulder.

I unfolded the letter and imagined Dominic's big hands folding the paper neatly, perhaps tucking it in his shirt pocket before getting it to me.

The letter was written in a large, simple scrawl.

Dear Benedetta,

I don't know why I said what I did. It was not right. It was stupid. I did not mean it. Sometimes I don't think about what I'm saying.

It is hard to live up here, and not see people all day. The only time I see anyone is at night, and then we sleep.

I think about you. All the time. Maybe you do not like me very much, but I like you. I hope you'll give me another chance. If you want to answer, leave a note under this same rock.

Dominic

P.S. Except that it is much prettier, your hand is no different than mine.

I put the letter down on the bed next to me, questions flooding my mind. How did he get the letter under the rock? Was someone acting as a messenger for the men in the mountain? Had someone from the village been to the mountain? Or, I shuddered to think, had he brought the note down himself? A two-hour walk one way, sneak up to the very house where the German soldiers were resting, all to leave a note for me? It just wasn't possible. Someone else from the village brought the note; it was the only realistic possibility.

I folded the letter and placed it in the small pocket at the front of my dress. This required a response. An immediate response.

I went to the small desk in the corner of the room and found a piece of paper. A half-chewed, stubby pencil showed itself from the back corner of the desk's drawer. A bird landed on the windowsill and cocked an eye at me. I looked back, wondering if it was going to tell me something, but then it flapped its wings and disappeared.

I put the pencil to the paper, but hesitated. I read over his letter again. He had been cautious. I did not want to say too much, but still needed to get the message across.

With my forehead resting in my left hand, I scratched out a message quickly. I wanted this to be from the heart. I read it over, used the eraser to change a word here and there, but for the most part it conveyed what I felt.

I folded the paper, then put it next to Dominic's letter in the front pocket of my dress.

"Iole," I called, going down the stairs. She appeared in an instant, welcoming the chance to avoid doing any more work in the kitchen. "Come with me."

We walked outside, behind the house, to the dilapidated barn. A low rock wall separated the barn from the empty field next to it. It was made of dark stone and had been here a long time. It had maybe formed part of a foundation for a building that had long since disappeared. The rocks were in neat rows, all of different shapes and sizes.

"Show me where you found the note," I said.

"Why?"

"Just show me."

"Are you answering him?"

"Iole, asking questions will just get you into trouble."

She was quiet for a moment, and we walked farther up the wall toward the forest beyond. "I'm certain it's right here."

Iole walked directly up to a section of the wall, hesitated, then moved a little bit past it. "Or was it here?" she said with a sly smile.

Quick as a cat, I had her ear between my thumb and forefinger. "Try to remember." Although the pressure was slight, she started squirming in anticipation. "Try a little harder," I said, squeezing a bit harder.

"There! There!" she said, pointing to a section of the wall that was no more than three feet from where we were standing. I followed her finger and saw the one rock that was jutting out, fresh moss exposed to the sunlight.

"That rock there?" I asked.

She nodded.

"Are you sure?"

"Yes, Benedetta. Don't worry; he'll find it."

I shot a sharp look at her and she moved a couple of steps away from me, toward the house.

"Go back to the house, and tell no one of this spot, or you'll be in so much pain, you'll wish the Germans were interrogating you!"

She ran back toward the house and I picked up the rock, placed my note in the empty space, then put the rock back on top of it. I left the rock tilted slightly out of line with the rest of the wall. Enough for Dominic to notice, but not so much that anyone else would without looking closely.

I stood and looked at the distance from the rock wall to the edge of the pine forest. Although I still believed that someone else brought the note for Dominic, that he wouldn't be foolish enough to risk coming down the mountain by himself just to give me a note, I did notice that the forest's edge was less than thirty yards from the stone wall. If Dominic had come, he could've walked down the path, skirted the village under cover of the woods, made it to the stone wall, then gone back the way he came.

I hoped, for his sake, that wasn't the case. I didn't want anyone risking his life to give me a love letter. In fact, I was almost angry with him for taking such a risk, for putting me ahead of himself. I did not want to be responsible for anyone's death; there had been far too much of it already.

But when I walked back to the house, some strange things happened. My legs suddenly felt lighter. There was a bounce in my step. And on my face was a big, happy smile.

CHAPTER TWENTY-SEVEN

—

L ate in the afternoon, a visitor came to the house.

Her name was Rosa Zanussi. She lived on the eastern side of Casalvieri; her husband had health problems and her only daughter was fully grown and married, off with a family of her own. She also had a son who had left Casalvieri many years ago and now lived in Naples.

Her husband had contracted polio and now walked with the aid of a walking stick and a cumbersome brace. His left arm was withered, ending prematurely in a stump with two fingers. For better or worse, he was safe during the war. Even the Germans could find no use for him.

Signora Zanussi was a woman who had lived a hard life. Secretly, a lot of the younger women in Casalvieri feared they would end up like her. And the truth was, many, if not most, would. She had probably never been a pretty woman, and the long days of tending crops and caring for her children as well as a crippled husband had all wreaked havoc on her body. She was prematurely old.

Her dress was stitched and restitched many times over. Strands of gray hair hung across her face and remained there, their owner too tired to make the effort to tuck them behind her ear.

"Good morning, Benedetta," she said, a half-formed smile on her face appearing and departing quickly, as if it knew it would never reach its full potential so just decided to quit ahead of time.

"How are you, Signora Zanussi?"

She looked down and shifted her feet. Her thick ankles were throbbing with varicose veins. "I am fine. God has not told me to join him today, so I will continue doing what I do for another day."

Finding a response to that proved impossible.

"Benny," she whispered, leaning close to me and looking around for people eavesdropping. "Do you know you have the only rooster left in Casalvieri?"

"That can't be!"

"It is true."

From the folds of her dress her hand emerged, holding four eggs. "I would like to rent him."

"What?" The war had proven ghastly, but now it was just getting downright weird.

"Our hen is ready; it is time. Without a rooster, well . . ."

"It is an opportunity not to be missed, no?" I answered.

She nodded emphatically. "She is our last hen, Benedetta. If she doesn't have chicks soon, who knows if she ever will."

"Your hen is probably one of the last in Casalvieri, too," I said.

"I don't know; I think people are hiding their animals from the Germans, but it isn't always easy."

I thought of the pig, a hundred yards away hidden in a secret compartment of the barn.

Signora Zanussi continued. "Who knows when the time will come again? Who knows what will still be alive in the next year?"

We both knew what she really meant.

"Come with me," I said.

I led her to the pen, where, perched imperiously on one leg, stood our rooster, Gallo.

Seemingly aware of his audience, he fluffed his neck feathers and strutted around the pen. I rolled my eyes at the sight of him. Auditioning for his role, perhaps?

"He senses why we are here," Signora Zanussi said, laughing.

I entered the pen and scooped him up. He bobbed his head back and forth, seemingly excited about the possibilities of what might lie ahead. For a moment I thought I could feel his heart beating wildly.

Signora Zanussi handed me the eggs and I handed her Gallo.

She stroked his feathers and he jutted his head forward, his neck rising to meet her hand. This was going to be good, he was probably thinking. He looked at me as if to say, "Wish me luck."

I kicked the door to the pen, and it closed with a solid clang.

"How is Signor Zanussi?" I asked.

"He is in great pain, Benedetta. And it will only get worse; at least that's what the doctors say."

"Our hearts go out to him."

She shrugged again. "We are all going to be in great pain, soon," she said. "Already the people of Casalvieri are starting to feel the beginning of the long hunger that will come. All food is running low. There is talk that other villages like Roselli and Scatozza may soon have to be evacuated."

"The Americans?" I said, not attempting to hide the hope in my voice.

"Yes, the Americans are making some advances south of here," she said. "These other villages, they will come here. They have to. And there is not enough food here for us as it is. What will happen when hundreds of new people start pouring into our town? Where will they get food to eat? Water to drink?"

"They will be even hungrier than us," I said.

Signora Zanussi's face was flushed. "Who knows, maybe they will try to take what little we have left." She shrugged. "You are safe here, Benny, with the Germans. There is always something good in bad, at least. Who in their right mind will try to take something from you? But what about me? I have a man who can barely walk; if hooligans want to rob me, how will I manage to stop them? Throw my empty pots and pans at them?"

She laughed in spite of herself.

"We must somehow try to make it through this together," I said. "The people of Roselli are no different than the people of Casalvieri. We cannot become each other's enemies. We have enough enemies as it is."

"You and I know that, Benny. But will their hungry stomachs know that?"

We were silent then, until I handed her back two of the four eggs.

"No, no . . ." she started.

"Take them. I do not need them all. They . . ." I said, gesturing toward the house, ". . . do not need them, either. Two is plenty for Iole and Emidio and myself. Take two back. Signor Zanussi needs them, too."

She reluctantly put two of the eggs back in the pocket of her dress.

"Besides," I said, gesturing toward Gallo, "he may act like a big man, but who knows if he'll actually get the job done?"

She laughed then and leaned closer.

"We must stay strong, Benedetta." She wrapped her hand around my hand that was still holding the two eggs. "Eat these for yourself and your brother and sister. You children need them for strength."

I looked down at her hands; the arthritic knuckles were turning white as she squeezed my hand.

"We will be here long after these *Germanesí* have gone," she said. "We must be strong enough to rebuild what they destroy. It is the way it has always been."

She left then, walking away with great effort, Gallo under her arm. His feet were moving, running hard and kicking but getting nowhere.

I knew the feeling.

CHAPTER TWENTY-EIGHT

—

Becher sat tight-lipped at the head of the table, a soldier on each side of him. Iole, Emidio, Zizi Checcone, and I took up the rest of the table.

Dinner consisted of yet another stew, this time made with meat that Zizi Checcone guessed was lamb, although she knew of no one in the area who had not butchered and eaten all of their sheep long ago. Bread and wine were also on the table.

Conversation around the dinner table typically consisted of the Germans talking among themselves, with the occasional call for more bread or wine. Usually, we sat in silence except for the occasional command to Iole and Emidio to eat what was in front of them, and to eat all of it. Even now, Iole continued to be a bit of a picky eater, though she had to have been ravenous.

Something was wrong with Becher. He seemed even more stern and humorless than usual. Although we couldn't follow the conversation between him and the soldiers, I could tell he wasn't happy about something. *Things must not be going well on the mountain*, I thought to myself.

I went to the pot over the fireplace to scrape any remnants from its sides while Zizi Checcone stepped outside to bring more bread from the oven. That left Iole and Emidio at the table with the Germans.

What happened next shocked me.

"Boy," Becher said to Emidio. "Bring me the wine."

Emidio reached up and took the bottle from the table. It was big in his hands and he carried it carefully. Just as he got to Becher, he tripped. Whether it was over the foot of the soldier next to Becher, or whether it was the soldier's chair, I do not know. But I do know that the wine flew from Emidio's hand and hit Becher squarely in the chest, where it proceeded to flow out over his uniform.

Becher jumped from his chair, reared back, and slapped Emidio across the face. My little brother flew backward and landed on his back.

"Stupid Italian bastard!" Becher shouted. He strode forward to Emidio, who was too stunned to start crying, lifted him to his feet by his shirt, and started slapping him—left, right, left, right, and back again. Emidio's head snapped with each blow.

I dropped the pot and ran to spring myself upon Becher. Coolly, he dropped Emidio, who fell in a heap sobbing, and drew his pistol. I stopped in front of Becher and he placed the muzzle of his pistol squarely against my forehead.

The door flew open and Zizi Checcone stood aghast at the scene before her. She quickly crossed the room and scooped Emidio up into her arms. I could see that his nose and mouth were bleeding.

"We are low on ammunition," he said, a half smile on his face. "Otherwise I would take great joy in blowing your brains across this house."

Iole started screaming, and Zizi Checcone went to her, scooped her up, and stood with a child in each arm.

"You are very brave when it comes to hurting children," I said.

"Benedetta," Zizi Checcone said.

Becher laughed. "You are very brave also, thinking that Colonel Wolff will protect you, perhaps?"

I said nothing. His pistol was still pressed against my forehead. He pushed harder.

"You are a stupid girl. You have no idea with whom you are dealing."

"I know." My voice was steady, my heart racing, blackness threatening to envelop me, but I knew, I could feel the violence within me, the desire to kill.

"Really," he said, pulling back the hammer of the gun. "Tell me who."

"An animal who cannot taste enough blood."

Zizi Checcone told me I was going to get us all killed. When she said that, the blackness receded, and I regained my senses. Becher pulled back his pistol and I knew he was going to strike me with it, but made no move to avoid the blow. If he succeeded in hurting me, maybe he would leave my brother and sister and Zizi Checcone alone.

When the pistol hit me, I felt a searing pain in the side of my face and the room whirled wildly, then crashed to a stop as the floor slammed up to meet me. It did not knock me out, but I lay still. When I heard his boot whisper on the floor, I thought I could hear the kick coming, and then it hit me in the stomach, the wind going from inside, and I could not breathe. I kept my eyes closed as I gasped for air, a soft moaning sound coming from somewhere deep within me. The kick turned me over, away from Becher and the other soldiers. I opened one eye and saw Zizi Checcone, Iole, and Emidio. I made eye contact with the old woman to let her know I was hurt, but still alive.

"The taste of blood has made me hungry," Becher said, and then I heard the scrape of his chair as he sat back down. The soldiers and Becher talked low, in German, and I stayed on the floor.

Zizi Checcone went up the stairs with Iole and Emidio, and then came back down alone.

She rolled me onto my back and I winced. I felt something trickling down my face and at first I thought it was tears, but Zizi Checcone wiped it and her hand came away red with blood. She went to the pot over the fireplace and returned with a warm, damp cloth, which she used to clean my wound.

"Can you stand?" she whispered. I nodded.

She helped me to my feet and again the room spun around me, tilted at a crazy angle. The conversation at the table stopped; I knew they were watching. With a thick arm around me, Zizi Checcone pushed me toward the stairs, but we stopped at the sound of Becher's voice.

"Benedetta," he said. "I still don't have my wine."

I turned with a monumental effort. He sat there, his empty glass raised toward me. Zizi Checcone let go of me and I stood by myself as she went and retrieved a full bottle of wine, then started toward Becher.

"Ah. Ah. No. Benedetta will do it."

Zizi Checcone stopped and stood halfway between Becher and me. In a whisper, she asked me if I could do it.

I nodded again.

With shooting pains in my head and now running up and down my spine, I walked to Zizi Checcone, then to Becher. The bottle shook in my hand and I slopped wine into his glass, nearly pouring it to overflowing, but I stopped just in time.

I brought the bottle back down and walked to Zizi Checcone. She took the bottle from my hand and helped me to the stairs.

"See?" Becher said. "Even a stupid girl can learn."

CHAPTER TWENTY-NINE

—

Two days later, with Emidio back to himself and my bruise reduced in size, the edges starting to turn yellow, I went to see Lauretta Fandella. She was working in the kitchen with her mother, cleaning a big black pot, when I knocked on the door.

She opened it and I was shocked by her appearance. Her skin looked pale and dry, like parchment paper, and her hair hung thick and oily, like it hadn't been washed in the last week or two.

"Benedetta," she said, a vacant look on her face. "Come in."

I went inside and Lauretta climbed the stairs, then came back down with a sweater.

"I'm going for a walk, Mama."

Her mother looked over her shoulder at us but didn't respond as we left the house.

"How are you, Benedetta?" she asked, and I told her about my trip up the mountain. I hadn't told Iole or Emidio anything about it, of course, and I didn't discuss it with Zizi Checcone, though I was certain she knew where I had been. I got the feeling she was scared to even whisper any mention of the men in the mountains. After all, we had Germans under the same roof.

Lauretta was someone in whom I could confide. So I told her about the walk up the mountain with Dominic, the trip to find the parachute, and I told her about the walk to the spring when I lost my temper.

She looked at me appraisingly.

"I'm impressed, Benedetta," she said. "A little surprised, but still I am impressed. So many Italian women let the men say what they want to them."

When I thought about the incident with Dominic, I was embarrassed, but the way Lauretta spoke about it, I almost felt a warm resurgence in my heart; I felt proud of what I had done.

I told her about the letter under the rock, as well.

"Dominic Giancarlo. I have heard of him. He is from Roselli, no?"

I nodded, feeling fear rush through me. How did she know of him? Did some of her girlfriends know him? Had they been with him? Did he have a reputation for being with lots of girls? I felt myself flush. I had never thought these kinds of things before.

"Yes, I have heard of him," Lauretta said.

"What do you know?"

"That many, many girls are in love with him, but he is a *lazzarone*. He likes to be with the men playing cards, drinking wine. Playing around. He dances, he flirts, but his mama is a strict woman and he does not fool around. At least that is what I hear."

Relief flowed through me. I knew she was telling me the truth, as much of it as she knew, and I was grateful for what she had told me.

"He is that way now, but there will come a time soon when women will be most important to him," she said. "And when that happens, there will be lots of girls ready for him."

I felt another emotion surge through me, this one powerful as well and all consuming. It was jealousy. I did not like how it made me feel.

"We will see what kind of man he is," I said. "When he gets my note and reads it, we will see."

"I think that you do not have anything to worry about, Benedetta. He does not sound like a skirt chaser."

I felt a surge of relief that I tried to hide. We walked past the village and out along the outskirts of town where there was a small park-like setting with some logs chopped down and arranged into sitting areas. We sat next to one another on a log.

A bird flew overhead and somewhere a dog was barking. The booming of the big guns reached us from the mountain.

I turned and looked at Lauretta. Her silence confused me; usually it was tough for me to work a word in edgewise. She looked at the ground, her eyes vacant.

"Lauretta, what is wrong?"

She looked at me, shook her head, then wrapped her arms around herself.

"Nothing, nothing's wrong."

"Lauretta, I know you too well."

She whispered something.

"What?"

"They found out," she said softly.

The guns stopped booming briefly. In the silence, I tried to figure out what she meant.

"Who?"

"Becher. Schlemmer."

I went cold inside. The guns started booming again and the wind picked up, a chill in the air.

"What did they find out, Lauretta?"

She looked at the ground a long time before answering. "My father."

"What about him?" I said.

"They found out about my father. Somehow. They did."

"That he . . ."

"That he's a *ribelli*. I think they caught him and a couple other men trying to blow up a truck. I think they killed him," she said.

"Did they say they did?"

"No, they said they haven't and . . ."

"And what?" I said.

"And they won't."

Suddenly, I knew. I wanted to stop; I didn't want to ask more questions and I didn't want Lauretta to tell me. But she did.

"They say they won't kill him if I let them . . . let them . . . do things to me," she said. She started crying.

"Have they . . ."

She nodded.

"They all have. All of them."

A strand of hair fell across her face. I tried to brush it back for her, but she jerked away from me.

"Don't touch me. I don't want anyone to touch me. Ever again."

We sat there.

"I want to die, Benedetta," she said. "I just want to die." Her lip trembled then, and she fell into my arms. I hugged her as tightly as I could and never wanted to let go.

CHAPTER THIRTY

—

The pig was getting fat.

It was amazing what a pig could eat and digest. This pig was gaining weight on coffee grounds, bones, and anything else unfit for human consumption.

I threw him some husks of corn, closed the chicken coop door and latched it, then moved the odds and ends in front of the door to disguise any signs of recent use; so far it had worked. It was a good hiding spot; no one would think that a sagging little structure set so far away from everything else would be housing a farm animal. And as far as I knew, this little guy was the only pig still alive in this part of the country.

Walking back to the house, it seemed that the air was getting colder, and I folded my arms, hugging my ragged sweater tightly to my chest.

In the kitchen, I could smell the menestra that was becoming our nightly meal. Zizi Checcone stood at the hearth and stirred the large pot. I looked inside; it was an even thinner soup than normal. Rations were getting lower every day.

Zizi Checcone saw the look in my eye and shrugged.

"It is not much, but it will warm the stomach," she said.

I gathered up some bowls as she carried the large pot to the big table. Several soldiers were already seated. Neither Colonel Wolff nor Becher had yet returned from the front. The soldiers were dirty and dazed, tired from fighting; they dug into the weak soup with relish.

Iole placed a small loaf of bread between them.

"*Grazie, grazie,*" they said to us, in appreciation for a warm meal, probably the first one they'd had in several weeks. The men were rotated to and from the front, spending a day or two here to rest and recover, then back to the fighting they went. It was quiet now in the house, even with the soldiers here. They were so tired, all they could manage to do was just sleep and eat. After the soldiers finished eating, we sat down and took their places, eating the rest of the soup and bread. Anger began to well up inside me when I saw that there was only one small piece of bread left. There would barely be enough for either Iole or Emidio, but not for both. There was no question that Zizi Checcone and I would go without.

But when Iole and Emidio sat down, Zizi produced three thick slabs of bread and a small square of butter. It had been a long time since we'd seen butter and now it sat there, beautifully golden in color.

"Eat, eat, quickly!" she snapped at us, fearful that the soldiers would return for another cup of wine and see more bread.

Like wolves around a carcass, we ate the bread as quickly as we could, at the same time trying to savor the presence of real butter—a true delicacy in this wasteland of death and hunger.

"How . . . ?" I started to ask, but the old woman shook her head.

Iole and Emidio did not ask from where the surprise had come; they kept their heads down and ate their soup in silence. I noticed the dark circles under their eyes, the wooden movements of their hands as they ate, and I wept inside. Their childhood was being destroyed along with the houses, the crops, and so many lives of the men from the villages. But was nothing worse, nothing harder to replace, than the joy of one's youth? Houses could be rebuilt, crops could be replanted, but once their innocence, their joy, was gone, I began to doubt if it could ever be replaced.

"Hey, you two," I said. "After we eat and clean up, I have another surprise for you upstairs."

Zizi Checcone looked at me questioningly.

We scrubbed the dishes—although it wasn't too hard to clean the pot in which a watery soup was made—wiped the table, swept the floor, and prepared the stove for a nice warm fire in the morning.

Zizi Checcone brought out needle and thread and began to mend some garments while I took Iole and Emidio upstairs. They bounded up behind me, peppering me with questions: "What's the surprise? What is it? Do you have a game? Come on, Benedetta, tell us! Tell us!"

I jumped on the bed and they followed, clambering over me. Finally, I set Emidio on my lap, and Iole sat across from us.

"Now, do you two know that I love you very much?" They rolled their eyes and fidgeted, anxious to get to the surprise. "Do you know that ever since Mama passed away, I've tried to do my best to take care of you?" They stopped fidgeting at the sound of Mama's name, and I felt a warmth come into my cheeks. "I just want you to know that all of this will be over one day, maybe even one day soon, and when that happens, Papa will come back and things will go back to the way they used to be. There will be good food on the table and plenty of happy times ahead."

They nodded that they understood, but I could tell they had their doubts, and I couldn't blame them; I had doubts, too. The Allies seemed stronger than Germany, but the Germans were committed. And even if the Germans were defeated, what would the Allies do with Italy? Our country was in league with Hitler, and

Mussolini was a Fascist. Would we be punished for taking up arms against the Allies, even if for most of us it had been against our will?

I pushed the thoughts from my mind. We would all have to do what it takes to survive. To dwell on what might happen would do nothing more than ensure an ulcer if one lived long enough to suffer. I intended to survive, and I intended for my family to not just survive as well, but to come out of all this in one piece, not like some of these soldiers: nothing more than ghosts living in human shells.

Iole and Emidio were looking at me, and I snapped out of my train of thought.

"Are you done daydreaming, Benedetta?" Iole asked. "Or are you just trying to make up an excuse for why you don't have a surprise for us?"

"I have a surprise. Let me get it for you."

From inside the top drawer of my dresser, I pulled a small cloth wrapped up into a tight square. I laid it on the bed, and Iole and Emidio's eyes were wide with anticipation.

"Here it is," I said, caressing the soft cloth.

"Open it! Open it!" Emidio said, leaning forward over the bundle like a deer about to drink from a stream.

"There's nothing in there; she's playing a trick on us," Iole said, her eyes riveted to the small package.

"Oh, really?" I said, lifting a corner of the cloth, then another and another and another.

"Then I suppose you won't be wanting any of this nothing, eh?" I said, lifting the final section of cloth.

They both inhaled sharply.

There, huddling together on the pristine white cloth backdrop, were two incredibly thick, incredibly large squares of American chocolate.

Iole started to reach for a square first.

"Eh, eh, eh!" I said.

She shot her hand back and they both looked at me again.

"Before I give them to you, you have to promise me a couple of things."

They nodded solemnly.

"You have to promise that you'll continue to help me and Zizi Checcone around the house."

"I promise," they said in unison.

"You have to promise that you'll never ask me where I got it."

"I promise."

"You have to remember that you are young and deserve to have fun, so promise me that every day you'll play bocci or chase each other or swing on the big tree out back."

They looked at each other like I had gone crazy. Benedetta ordering them to play? It didn't seem possible.

"I promise," they repeated in unison.

"And finally, promise that you'll give me hugs and kisses before you dig in," I said. They giggled and showered me with hugs and kisses.

"Enough! Enough! Eat! Enjoy!" I pushed them off and they reached with reverence for their respective squares. As they bit into the sweet candy, I didn't believe I had ever seen such ecstasy as I saw then in their eyes; they savored the rich chocolate like it was a forbidden desire at last indulged.

As they ate the chocolate, and then licked their fingers, I idly stroked their hair, marveling at the smoothness of their skin, the delicacy of their features. They were growing up fast. Even in the middle of a war without enough food to go around, they were still growing up too fast.

I knew all too well what it was like to have a childhood cut short. If there was a way to prevent it from happening to them, by God, I was going to find it.

CHAPTER THIRTY-ONE

—

Two days later, the next note came.

I was in the habit of stopping by the low stone wall several times a day, more than I'd like to admit, but it was true—there was a lightness in my stomach, a tightening of my throat when I came close to where the loose rock was. When there was nothing underneath it, I felt a mixture of sadness and relief. A lack of love sometimes makes life simpler.

But on a crisp morning when the dew was still on the grass and the sun was just beginning to make its presence felt and layering warmth on my back, I saw the white of paper peeking out from beneath the chosen stone.

I checked over my shoulder and scanned the surrounding field as well as the edge of the forest. No one was around. The Germans were still sleeping, and Iole, Emidio, and Zizi Checcone had walked to the other side of town, where a friend of Zizi Checcone supposedly had some extra zucchini with which she was willing to part.

I had told them I was going to stay at the house and get breakfast started, and that I also needed to go out back to the bread oven to make sure the sealing clay was still affixed around the door, but I knew I wasn't fooling anyone. Iole certainly had an idea what was going on, and Zizi Checcone probably did, too. She didn't miss much.

I lifted the rock and picked up the letter underneath, but then I saw a second note underneath the first.

The first letter was heavily wrinkled, with small grease spots along one side. Dominic had resorted to using bits of wrap from something as a substitute for paper. "Benedetta" was written across the top in the same loopy scrawl as his first letter.

I unfolded it, and imagined that I could smell the smokiness of the cabin, the men cramped into that tiny space, the smell of cards on the table and weak coffee brewing over the fire.

It started off simply.

Benedetta,

Your letter made me happy. Thank you for forgiving me. We were with each other for a short time, but my feelings are strong. Not a day, not an hour, not a minute goes by that I do not think of you.

I am not good with words, but I feel that nightingales whisper your name, and the chambers of my heart resonate with their song.

I miss you.

Dominic

P.S. To answer your question, I bring the notes myself.

The last line hit me like a sledgehammer. Foolishly, I looked to the trees, half-expecting to see him there, waving at me, smiling. I would rush into his arms and we would fall together to the forest floor, in each other's arms, kissing. But that could not be; he would not remain here during the day—it was too dangerous. He would walk down the path at night, leave the note, then walk back up the mountain. At night, in the mountains, the land reverts back to the Italians.

I bring the notes myself. I read it again, horrified and warmed at the same time. This man, this young man, was risking his life to communicate with me, to express his feelings. No one had ever done anything like that for me before. Sure, there had been flirtatious young men, but theirs was meaningless chatter, all talk to impress other young men. They made up lies and inflated their chests, but they were still boys. Dominic. Now Dominic was different.

The words themselves even reminded me of him—simple, to the point, saying a lot with a little. Relief came over me in waves. He was not frightened off by my losing my temper with him at the spring. He was a man who could handle a strong woman; that was good.

I picked up the second letter. My name was on the front, too, but in a different handwriting. I recognized the penmanship: It was my father's.

Dearest Benedetta,
I love you with all my heart; I know you know that. I want nothing but the best for you. I know Dominic is bringing letters to you. I had him bring this one. I trust this young man; I know he didn't read it. He is a good boy. But I do not want you to get involved with him. I will tell you later why. Please respond to him that you are not interested, or I will do it myself.
I am sorry, Benedetta. But that is how it must be.

Give my love to Iole and Emidio.
Your Papa

Like Dominic's, I read the letter again. *Why would Papa want me to stop talking to Dominic, especially if he thinks he's a good boy?* I was not too young; lots of girls my age were starting to develop friendships with boys. There was nothing wrong with what I was doing. And why was he being so mysterious about why? Why would he tell me later?

I crumpled both notes into the front pocket of my dress and headed back for the house. This was too much. I was being torn between my father and the man I now knew I was in love with.

Nothing was ever easy. I had allowed myself a simple dream, one in which Dominic and I were married after the war, our families joining us in celebration, and then we would start a family. I momentarily forgot, impossible as it seemed, the war around us. I had thought there would be nothing standing in our way. And now this, a letter of disapproval from my father, a man who loved and cared about everyone. *How could this be?*

I stormed toward the house, seething with frustration. As I got closer, I heard screams and crying. Running with images leaping to my mind of Iole and Emidio being shot or stabbed, I came upon the house and now could tell that the crying was coming from Zizi Checcone. I rounded the corner and Iole and Emidio, ashen faced, were in Zizi Checcone's arms as she sobbed uncontrollably.

"What? What is it?" I cried.

Iole and Emidio jumped out of her arms and ran to mine.

"We couldn't see," Iole said. "Someone . . ."

Zizi Checcone walked slowly toward me, tears streaming down her face.

"Someone what?" I said.

"It is your friend, Lauretta," Zizi Checcone said.

"What happened to Lauretta?" I said, my heart filling with dread. Zizi Checcone's face was red as tears continued to pour.

"The Germans . . ."

"What are they doing to her? Where is she?" I could hear my voice rising to panic.

Zizi Checcone opened her wide arms and started to hug me.

"They have hung her."

CHAPTER THIRTY-TWO

—

The streets, the trees, the houses, the faces along the way were a teary blur to me. My feet felt wooden as I ran. My face was wet but I wasn't crying; my eyes were wide open and unblinking. I pictured arriving in time to lift Lauretta down, explain that it was all a mistake, and nurse her back to health so we could go back to the clearing in the woods and watch the American pilot wave to us again. I would tell her that we had made it this far, that she just couldn't die on me now; it was too close to the end. And then she would open her eyes and I would help her back to her room where we would lie on her bed and look at Enrico Caruso.

People were dispersing from a group at the center of town, hurrying away and crossing themselves in prayer. I pushed my way through them to the front.

The world dropped from beneath my feet.

She was dead.

There was no doubt in my mind as I saw her body hanging limply from a wooden beam.

Lauretta's neck was stretched to twice its normal length, a grotesque sight that I knew would forever be burned into my memory. She didn't look human with her neck like that; she looked like a painting in which the artist exaggerated the subject's features. Her head was tilted down and to the side; her face was pale and her eyes stared sightlessly over the tops of the trees toward the distant hills.

Her feet were pointed outward, both shoes missing. I wondered if they'd been stolen. Her dress was the same one I had last seen her in: a green print with yellow flowers and patches worn smooth and shiny from use. There was blood on the dress, from what, I did not want to think.

"Cut her down," I said to no one in particular, not sure if I had even said the words out loud.

No one responded, but a few people in the crowd moved away from me.

"Cut her down."

Two German soldiers, stationed inside the abandoned store, sauntered out and stood to either side of the body.

One of them was Schlemmer. He gestured to Lauretta's body, which was twisting slowly in the gentle breeze.

"*Ribelli*," he sneered. "For three days she must hang here, so the rest of you know what will happen if you fight us."

"Cut her down!" My voice was high and unsteady. I could hear people behind me moving farther away, not wishing to be in the line of fire if it should come to that.

"Her father and some other men bombed a supply truck, killing the driver. This is what happened as a result of that," he said.

"Who ordered her to be hanged? Colonel Wolff? He would not do such a thing."

"Becher understands how we need to treat you filthy people," Schlemmer said. The other soldier laughed.

"Filthy?" I asked. "Is that why you had so much fun with her before you killed her?"

The smile dropped from his face.

"Cut her down, *capibile*," I spat. "It is enough."

Schlemmer laughed and looked at the other soldier, who was shaking his head. Fury rose up inside me and I stepped up to Lauretta and took hold of her feet, which were ice cold. I hugged them to my chest anyway. The rope had been tied over the thick post supporting the sign, then trailed down and was tied off to a stanchion against the wall.

I let go of Lauretta's feet and stepped forward to untie it.

The hard heel of Schlemmer's boot caught me just above my stomach, in the midriff and lower part of my rib cage. I fell backward into the street, landing on my back, my head crashing onto the hard dirt, the air escaping from my lungs with a whoosh.

It took a minute to focus, and I had a flashback to when Becher had done the same thing. But this time, I would fight back.

I threw my weight forward and bounced up, then rushed him, ready to tear the flesh from his face with my bare hands.

Schlemmer kicked me again, harder this time, directly in the stomach. I sank to my knees and he grabbed my hair in his fist and dragged me back into the street. The second soldier followed, kicking me in the legs, thighs, and bottom.

A blind fury seized me and I twisted and clawed, kicked, and swung my arms.

I felt hands pin my arms behind my back as Schlemmer stepped back and slapped me hard across the face. The second slap didn't sting as much as the first. After the third and fourth, I felt almost nothing. The taste of blood seeped into my mouth. It was starting to become a familiar flavor.

The arms released me and I dropped to the ground. New hands,

162

gentler this time, scooped me up underneath the arms and pulled me away.

"This is your friend, girl?" Schlemmer's voice taunted. I looked up at him through a veil of blood and tears. My eyes bored into his, and I studied every inch of his face, willing it into my memory so that when the day came, I knew I would be killing the right man.

He lifted his rifle and its steely bayonet glistened in the light. With a backward glance at me to make sure I was watching, a joyously giddy expression overcame his face as he reared back and then thrust forward, sinking the blade deeply into Lauretta's stomach. I closed my eyes but I had seen everything I needed to see. Pure, raw evil was before me, had touched me, had killed my best friend.

Her body was pushed backward, and Schlemmer withdrew the blade from her stomach.

Her face remained unchanged, but her body swung lightly; the rope chafed against the wooden beam and made a soft, squeaking sound.

Blackness descended across my eyes, through my heart, and over my soul.

CHAPTER THIRTY-THREE

———

The darkness remained, for how long I'm not sure, but Casalvieri never seemed to be such a dark, evil place as the days after the public execution of Lauretta Fandella. The body was removed, but the stench that hung over our small town would remain forever; the image of my best friend hanging in tribute to the authority of the Germans would never leave my mind. I knew from the minute I made my way through the crowd that what I would see would change my life forever.

Life at the house returned to the routine. Baking what little bread we could muster from the scant supplies. Laundry, cleaning, caring for Iole and Emidio went on. It always would, no matter what happened.

Fatigue grew rapidly on Zizi Checcone. It had been a long time since she'd cared for small children, and the daily hassles that Iole, Emidio, and sometimes even I created were draining her of energy. I tried to take over more responsibility for the cooking and especially the cleaning, but she was a tough old woman and wanted no help from any of us.

It was a midafternoon on a cold day when Colonel Wolff returned from the front. It had been almost a week since the murder of Lauretta, and several weeks since he'd left Casalvieri. The trucks pulled up to the front of the house, and the men entered wearily; some of them were injured and wore makeshift bandages. Their uniforms were filthy and most of them were covered in mud and smelled like rotten meat.

They assembled at the big table, where Zizi Checcone and I served them menestra and bread, which they ate with abandon, raising the bowls up and drinking any remaining soup. There was a small hunk of cheese that we placed on a cutting board at the center of the table. A small flask of wine managed to produce enough for each of the men to have a small glass.

Wolff came in the door walking slowly, his boots shuffling across the floor. His uniform was covered in dust and dirt, his face was ashen, and dark bags hung underneath his eyes. His shoulders were even more stooped than when I'd last seen him.

"Benedetta."

I stood in front of him and said nothing.

"Would you help me get my boots off?" he said as he wearily sat down.

He put his foot up on the chair next to him and I tugged them off, then set them on the floor next to him.

"How are you?" he asked.

"If you don't need me for something else, I'll get more soup for your men," I said, ice in my voice.

"Do that, then come back here and talk to me."

Zizi Checcone put out two more bowls of soup and I took them to the table. Wolff gestured for me to sit. As the men began finishing their meals, they went to their room to sleep.

"What is wrong with you?" he asked. "What are those marks on your face?"

"Your men take great joy in beating up children. Even killing them."

He looked at me tiredly.

"I'm not as used to death as you," I continued. "That is the problem."

"What are you talking about?"

"Your men hanged my best friend. One even stabbed her in the stomach after she was dead."

He slurped the soup loudly.

"I heard of this happening," he said. "I am sorry."

"I can tell."

Wolff looked like he was going to respond, but then said nothing. One by one, the last two men finished their soup and finally got up from the table.

"Believe me. If I had been here, it would not have happened. But understand, the girl's father was caught killing Germans," Wolff said. "You remember what I told your father when I first came here?"

I nodded, but he continued anyway.

"For every German that dies, ten of you die. Luckily, many of the *ribelli* with her father's band were killed. But Becher felt that an example needed to be set. Truly, I am sorry."

There was nothing left for me to say. These *Germanesi*, even the ones who maybe once had feelings, who maybe once knew the value of a life, had lost it by now. There was no hope, no chance that sympathy and compassion could be learned. If you had it, you had it. If you lost it, it was gone. It was that simple. I would remember this lesson. It was the kind of lesson you instantly know you will use for the rest of your life, no matter what the situation or the predicament. It gives you the kind of knowledge and perspective that will always be a part of your thinking.

"She was so innocent," I started to stay, but stopped. It wasn't something I wanted to talk about, but there it was.

"No one is innocent when his or her country is at war," Wolff said, mopping up the rest of his soup with a hunk of bread. "Once the leaders of a country say it's time to fight, everyone they govern is a participant."

I thought of Lauretta hanging from her neck. She was innocent. She would always be innocent as long as my memory and I survived. I would remember the Lauretta I knew all along. The one who dreamed of a man who would love her. The Lauretta created by the Germans had been hanged to death, gone forever.

I cleared the table and heard Wolff rise and make his way to his room. He moved slowly and loudly. I tried to picture him as a young boy in a German army, the first time he fired a rifle, the first time he watched someone die. His big blue eyes wide, watching blood pour onto the ground. He would have cried, I suspected. He was that kind of person.

There was a little bit of weak coffee left in the pot and I poured myself a cup, then sat at the big table. I ran my hand over the countless nicks and gouges in the wood, the wood my mother used to oil from time to time. She and my father must have had thousands of conversations right over this table.

I just wanted it all to be over. I wanted the Germans to pack up and leave, scared off by the Americans and British. I wanted Papa to come back, the men to go back to the fields, Lauretta to be alive again. I wanted my mother to come back to me, the baby to be all right, and for all of us to be one big happy family again.

The image of my father's face the way he looked in the mountains came back to me. There was no way to slow down his aging. One day, he would pass, too, and like now, there would be nothing I could do about it. If only I could raise my hand, shout "Stop!" and have the world put on hold while I went about making adjustments. A little push here, a little help there, and things would be different; things would be right.

I emptied the rest of the coffee into the sink. It didn't taste good; there was a sour taste in my mouth.

CHAPTER THIRTY-FOUR

—

The weeks dragged on, several months passed, and then spring came. The flowers along the edge of town began to show the tips of their white blossoms, throwing off a false, hypocritical light of gaiety.

Dominic's letters arrived in the same place every week. The first few were short and to the point, not straying far from the expected—"How are you?" "I miss you," "It's lonely up here"—to clichéd descriptions of the weather. But with each letter, he seemed to become more confident, more willing to express his feelings, as if writing about his emotions seemed to simultaneously make him more aware of them.

It was hard for me to believe that the young, shy boy I'd first met walking up the mountain had managed to transform himself into something of a poet, but it was true. I felt that his words, his willingness to stray beyond the first traditional proclamations of affection for me, were symbolic of how he was reaching out to me. Yes, sometimes he did fall into cliché, maybe he was even a bit sappy at times, but behind the words themselves the meaning was genuine, and I felt that honesty; I responded mentally and physically to the beauty of his truth.

I knew my father would not approve of the letter writing—he had told me, after all, to stop—but I did not care. No one was being harmed. Besides, I could tell Papa that we were just friends, even though I hoped it wasn't true.

I believed in following my heart, and my heart was leading me to Dominic. I answered his letters, his assertions of love, with my own.

Still, my father and mother always said I had a strong head on my shoulders and it was my head, not my heart, that began to suggest there was something wrong with the letters. Something about the way Dominic began with simple sentences and then switched to more flowery words. Even though I knew the sentiments being expressed were his own, I began to wonder if the actual words used to express them were.

I went to my father's room and looked at his bookcase. Not sure of what I was looking for, I scanned the titles on the shelf. There were some textbooks from his schooling so long ago. Father had only made it to the fifth grade before Nonna pulled him out and sent him to work in the fields. There were also a few picture books and a volume of poetry. Nothing seemed to stir my memory.

It was then that I remembered Luigi Iacobelli.

Without stopping to consider what I was doing, I walked out of the house and struck out for Luigi's house.

Signor Iacobelli had once wanted to be a priest, and had attended a prestigious seminary in Rome, but he had grown tired of the priesthood. There were rumors that he had left the church with abandon, living a decadent lifestyle for several years before returning to Casalvieri. He had the largest book collection in town, and people who needed to know something often went to his house to look something up on his bookshelves; in essence, he was the town's library.

I also knew that many young men went to his house; there was rumored to be a secret bookshelf that even Signora Iacobelli did not know about. There were supposed to be books that had things in them, scandalous things, things that would get a young boy like Luigi kicked out of the seminary.

I reached the Iacobelli house and knocked upon the front door. The house was a small, lopsided structure made of stone with a long grapevine winding its way around the walls, like a green snake bringing fresh fruit to its next victim.

The door opened and Signora Iacobelli smiled at me.

"Benedetta! Come in; come in. How are you?"

"Good, Signora. And you?"

"We're just fine, just fine. What can I do for you, girl?"

"Actually, I'm here to see Signor Iacobelli."

"Ah, you need to look something up, no?" Without waiting for a reply, she yelled toward the back of the house. "Gigi! You have a visitor."

Excusing herself to return to the kitchen, Signora Iacobelli left me standing there, silent in the front entryway before a small oil painting hanging crookedly on the wall. It was a picture of a young girl and a young man standing back-to-back beneath a tree.

"You like it? I bought it in Rome."

I turned to see Signor Iacobelli watching me from the hallway. He was in a wheelchair, a stump where his left leg should have been.

"It's nice."

"What can I do for you?" he asked.

"I'm looking for a book . . ."

"You have come to the right place. Follow me."

We went back down the hallway, passed the main room of the house, then turned left and went into a small room that was crowded with books from floor to ceiling. The bookshelves covered every wall and they were overflowing. Stacks of books were piled in corners and on tables. It was a mess.

"Now, what kind of book were you looking for?"

"A book of letters. Love letters." I felt myself blush.

Signor Iacobelli seemed to ponder that for a moment, and eyed me closely.

"I don't think I can help you with that one, Benedetta."

There was an awkward silence.

"Do you not have it, or can you not help me?"

I watched him closely and he dropped his gaze. "I may have had a book like that at one time . . ."

"Did a young man borrow it?"

He shrugged and held his hands out. "So many people borrow books from me, it is hard to keep things straight—as you can see."

My heart sank. He was not going to help me. I started to thank him for his time, but then a thought came to me.

"My brother will be so disappointed," I said.

"Your brother?"

"Yes, Emidio has a crush on a little girl, and he asked me to write her a love letter. I had heard that you might have a book of these things."

"But Emidio is so young!" the old man said.

"A young romantic," I corrected.

He laughed heartily and clapped his hands together.

"Ah, yes, I was young myself once, and in love. I was in love so many, many, many times." He chuckled and seemed lost in delicious thought for a moment, a small smile on his face.

At last, he faced me. "Now, what I said, Benedetta, was that I might have had such a book. That is true. But the men in the mountains, they need to write letters home to their girls, and some of them came and got it from me."

I knew then that I had my answer, but I could not stop now.

"However," he said quietly, looking over my shoulder to make sure Signora Iacobelli was not listening, "for some of my more, how shall we say, provocative works of literature, I do have copies, just in case the original gets . . . appropriated. Wait here."

He pushed himself into a small closet in the corner of the room and lifted something. I heard wood scraping; Signor Iacobelli grunted as he lifted a heavy object, then rummaged around. After much effort, he replaced the object, then closed the closet door.

When he came out, there were beads of perspiration on his forehead.

"Here we are. But be careful with it; it is my last copy."

I glanced down quickly. *Letters of Love.*

"Thank you. Emidio will be so happy."

I raced home and went directly to my room. I read the first few pages and nothing struck me, but on the fourth page I recognized this passage:

nightingales whisper your name, and the chambers of my heart resonate with their song

As I read on, more and more of the words were the same words Dominic had used in his letters. While I was not seized by an insane fury—after all, I still felt that the emotion he was expressing was genuine, and it was not uncommon for men to look for help in writing flowery letters—still, I started to get warm, as a slow anger rose within me. I thought of Lauretta, so much wiser in the ways of young men than I. She probably would have not been surprised by something like this. She probably would shrug and say, "That's what men do."

But I was different. I had not expected something like this, as obvious as it now seemed to me.

I got out a piece of paper and a pen, scribbled a short note, and walked out to the rock wall. I lifted the stone, hesitated, then opened my letter again to read it.

Dominic,
Your last letter was so warm and heartfelt, I know you love me so much to say these words straight from your heart. You have no idea how it makes me feel to know that a man of your honesty and integrity loves me.

I get weak at the knees thinking about it.

In fact, I don't think I can go on writing, so instead of trying to put anything down, why don't you turn to page 46 of your book for the rest of my letter.

Love,
Benedetta

I slipped the note under the rock and pushed it back into the wall.

CHAPTER THIRTY-FIVE

—

In early March, Mt. Cassino fell to the Allies, but only briefly. When the bombs started falling closer to Casalvieri, we knew something was wrong. When the first armored vehicles of the *Germanesi* roared down the mountain and into town, with the sounds of the bombs not far behind, we knew that the Americans had finally managed to top the mountain.

Boom-boom, boom-boom, KA-BOOM! Each explosion brought more Germans into town and they struggled to organize themselves. They looked like rats pouring out of a hole that was filling with gasoline. The town was instantly deserted, and for good reason. For months, rumors had floated around that the Germans would massacre the village before leaving, a rumor that was followed immediately by old women crossing themselves, as if the ritual would prevent a few more murders in the midst of an ocean of death and destruction.

As far as I knew, I was the only one looking forward to the fall of Mt. Cassino. The tension for me had been unbearable. I couldn't stand the thought of the Germans being in my house for one more week, let alone a month or even a year. No matter what kind of horror their retreat would bring, I felt joy at the prospect. Perhaps I would pay for that, but I was prepared to accept the price, come what may.

With a group of German soldiers parked in front of the house, Colonel Wolff finally pulled up in his jeep, and motioned his radio operator to follow him inside. The operator put the mobile radio on the big table, and I bustled about, getting coffee for Wolff and the radioman. Wolff sat down heavily as the operator set about powering up the radio and adjusting the frequency dial.

I set a cup down in front of Wolff and he drank half in one big gulp, seeming not to notice me or the fact that the coffee was hot to the point of scalding. There was a battle for control of Wolff's emotions: One minute he looked to be in an utter state of panic, the next minute a dull resignation, an acknowledgment of sin.

The radio squawked to life, and Wolff began barking short, guttural sentences in German into the microphone. A man's voice answered, surrounded by the sounds of bombs dropping, rifles firing, and heavy machinery grinding away.

After listening, Wolff spoke for several minutes, gesturing with his hands to the man on the other end of the radio, who could not possibly see them. I gathered that he was giving directions to his troops. When he finished, the radio squawked again and the man asked several more questions, to which Wolff responded with more sharp words and hand gestures. Finally, the man answered in the affirmative, Wolff nodded to the operator, who promptly turned the radio off and checked his watch, probably ready for an update at a certain preset time.

Wolff stood and walked outside, where he spoke to the men waiting for orders. They instantly hopped into their vehicles, and headed slowly back toward the mountain.

He came back inside, sat in the same chair next to the radio, leaned back, and ran his hand through his thick hair. His eyes fell on me.

"Benedetta, could I please have some more coffee?" he asked.

I filled his cup but his eyes were locked on mine.

"Benedetta, what will you do after the war?"

I thought for a moment.

"Starve," I said.

The radio operator laughed out loud. Wolff smiled, a movement that was weak and weary.

"When the Americans take over," Wolff started, and the radio operator shot him a look of disapproval. "It will happen one day, Klaus. We will not be here forever." The operator looked back to the radio and pretended to make some adjustments.

"When they take over, they will bring food, enough to get you to the planting season," Wolff said. "And you will have crops again, you will have wine, and the men from the mountains will return. You will be all right."

"You are more optimistic than I. There are stories that the village will be butchered."

Wolff rolled his eyes. "Ah, you Italians, you have such active imaginations. That's why you have so many artists and sculptors. It's all up here," he said, tapping the side of his head.

"Yes, I know what you mean," I answered hotly. "My friend Lauretta had a terrific imagination."

"Lauretta?"

"The girl that was hanged in the square."

He looked down at the table, visibly stung. He sipped slowly from his coffee cup, measuring his words. "There's that Italian fire, too," he said.

Just then, the radio blared, and the operator hurriedly adjusted the frequency knobs until the voice on the other end, screaming maniacally in German, came in loud and clear.

Wolff shouted into the microphone and the voice calmed. The two spoke back and forth, the operator hanging on every word, and a smile slowly spreading across his face.

After several minutes, Wolff jumped up and ran out the door, barked orders at the few men remaining outside, and then came back into the house. He picked up the microphone and spoke for several more minutes. At last, he nodded to the operator, who shut off the radio and stood, stretched, and clapped his hands.

Wolff smiled, too, but I got the sense that it was forced.

The operator said something and left. Wolff looked at me and I raised an eyebrow.

"The Americans accidentally dropped bombs on their own men. We were in full retreat, and they wiped themselves out. My men are going back in, killing the survivors. We have reclaimed the mountain. The Mignano Gap and Mt. Cassino are back in the hands of the Wehrmacht." There was no smile on his face, no look of triumph.

My heart sank and I turned my back on him, even though I got the sense he may have been just as disappointed as I. So much for Casalvieri returning to normal, so much for feeling safe, for being able to go to bed at night knowing that nothing terribly unspeakable will wake you up to the sound of screaming and gunfire.

"It looks like we will be here for a while longer."

I poked the fire listlessly.

"I'll make more coffee."

CHAPTER THIRTY-SIX

—

The ax blade severed the rooster's head with one clean stroke. Blood spurted onto the wood chopping block and I stepped back as he took off running, speeding around in tight circles. At last, he reversed direction, stood uncertainly swaying, then collapsed onto his side.

The decision had not been easy, and it was not made by me alone. Zizi Checcone had brought it up.

"It is time," she had said, gesturing toward the henhouse, now empty except for the gigolo.

"Time for what?"

"Your little brother and sister need protein. No one has rented Gallo for some time, probably because eggs are too precious at this point, even if it means fewer hens down the road. Everyone is living in the present. We must, too."

I walked to the bottom of the stairs.

"Emidio! Come here!"

Zizi Checcone watched me from the kitchen. Emidio walked down the stairs as if it was a struggle to do so. I scooped him up into my arms and looked at his face closely. There were dark circles under them, and I noticed red in the corners. I pulled his lips apart and looked at his teeth. I set him down and pulled his sleeves up, looking at his skin. There were several bruises on each arm.

"Where did you get these?" I asked, my temper rising.

"From chores."

"What chores gave you these?"

"Gathering wood, helping with the laundry."

"Go back upstairs."

Without a word I walked out of the house to the barn, where I got the small hatchet.

Emidio had never bruised that easily before. Zizi Checcone was right—something had to be done.

The rooster was happy to see me, figuring that I was either going to feed him or set him up on another romantic outing with one of his girlfriends. He strutted before me, full of bravado and self-confidence.

"You finished your life in style, rooster," I said. "That's more than a lot of us might be able to say."

Now I stood with his dead body in my hand. I hung him high in the barn, where no animal could get to him. In the morning, I would pluck him and boil him, then give the heart and liver to Iole and Emidio. They would no doubt complain, but they would eat the protein-rich parts or have them stuffed down their throats. They needed their strength. It's when you are young that your brain needs fat and protein for development; I would not let the *Germanesí* create any permanent damage to my little brother and sister.

I went back into the house, where Zizi Checcone motioned me to follow her. We walked back outside and around to the back of the house. She turned to me, and her black eyes were blazing.

"Here, take this to the pig." She handed me a large bucket with a towel over it. "If things continue, we are going to need to slaughter him in secret, and eat him ourselves—none for them," she said, gesturing toward the house with a look of contempt on her face.

"What's in it?" I asked. The pail was heavy. I couldn't think of any scraps we had that would weigh so much.

"Look once you get into the shed. Not before then," she said. "When you do, remember, war changes everything. We have to survive first. Now, go, and don't stop and talk to anyone."

She walked quickly back toward the house and I went to the barn. Once inside, I set the pail down and went to the back, moved all of the objects away from the wall, then brought the bucket back over.

I lifted the towel.

A severed hand sat on top. I jumped back, stifling a scream. My stomach surged and I felt vomit rise in the back of my throat, but I forced it down. A foul odor rose from the bucket and I moved farther away from it, then made the sign of the cross over my chest.

"Jesus, Mary, and Joseph," I whispered. Where did Zizi Checcone get this? I stepped forward and looked inside the bucket. Underneath the hand, I could see other hands, parts of a foot, maybe even a section of leg. And then the answer came to my mind. Of course, Zizi Checcone was very close with Signora Ingrelli, who was in charge of the makeshift hospital that had been set up in her home. Signora Ingrelli must have given these amputated limbs to her, probably because Zizi Checcone told her about the pig.

Were they crazy? Did they really think we would eat a pig that had been fed on the body parts of German soldiers?

The more important question was, now what? I couldn't just leave the bucket sitting here. I couldn't take it back to the kitchen and discuss what to do with its contents.

That's why she wanted me to wait until I was in the barn to look inside the bucket. Behind the house, I could have refused, and then she would have been left with this gruesome picnic basket. But now that I had it in here, I knew what I had to do. It was very crafty of her, and I admit I felt a grudging admiration for her. But now, I knew there was only one option, one thing left to do.

Feed the pig.

I opened the secret door and the pig scurried to the back corner. It stunk in the confined space, what with the close quarters and no fresh air.

He had stopped gaining weight, and it looked like he may have gotten a little thinner.

I stepped into the center of the small space, held the bucket as far away from me as possible, then turned it over. Hands, feet, ankles, and maybe even chunks of leg and arm plopped onto the dirt floor. I looked back in the bucket and a severed big toe was stuck in the middle of a drying pool of blood. I could see the long toenail, slightly yellow at the outer edge. There was dirt underneath the toenail, and dirt was caked in the folds of skin at the knuckle.

I shook the pail harder, but it didn't move. Looking around, I found a stick and pried the toe loose. It fell on top of the pile before bouncing off and rolling to the side.

I hurriedly stepped back and closed the door. Chills raced up and down my back and I again felt the urge to vomit. I pushed the old tub and the plowing harness back in front of the door. Along with some odd scraps of leather as well as a few pieces of old lumber, the catchall pile provided a good disguise for the secret door. I was careful once again to leave no trace of my presence. As I started to leave, I heard the pig grunting, and I knew he was eating. I didn't want to picture the scene—fingers and toes disappearing into the pig's mouth—but I couldn't help it. I knew one thing for certain. Never, under any circumstances, would I eat any part of this pig, no matter how hungry I became.

The bucket would need to be cleaned. I went to the well and rinsed it out, but I absolutely would not scrub it. Signora Ingrelli could do that. I had done enough already.

CHAPTER THIRTY-SEVEN

—

In the evening, a cool rain began to fall. It was one of those early spring rains that reminded everyone summer was still a way off, and that the remaining chill of winter would take its own sweet time in exiting.

My father's thick wool jacket kept me warm; a wide-brimmed hat made sure the rain didn't get down the back of my neck. I had taken to walking in the evenings, after the meals were cooked, the dishes cleaned, the laundry drying by the fireplace. The pretense of going for a walk had just been a ruse to check the rock wall for notes from Dominic, but I had begun to look forward to getting out of the house, breathing in fresh air, and looking at the stars. The work was always too much, and left me exhausted, but I found that I slept better after a walk.

The grass was wet, so I stepped carefully, not wanting the water to drench through to my socks too quickly. Out of the house, I turned right, walked past the barn toward the woods, and stopped at the same spot along the rock wall where the words of love had been placed for me, to fill my heart and my life with this new, strange thing.

Dominic had not answered my last letter. I worried that it had been too sharp, too cutting, but then again, I felt that he deserved it. If he didn't feel the confidence to write to me in his own words—well, that was no excuse. Cracked slabs of concrete do not make a proper foundation, nor do false words. He needed to learn that, or nothing of any kind of permanence could be built between the two of us. Nothing that could stand the test of time and endure life's harsher elements.

The stone was loose; a faded yellow splash of color struggled to peek around its oppressor. I looked over my shoulder. No one was near. I lifted the rock and opened the paper quickly, then held it tightly against my chest to make sure the rain didn't obliterate the message before I could read it. It was a short, terse message.

Benedetta,
Meet me in the Varano barn tonight. The words will be my own.

Love,
Dominic

I quickly read it again, as if I didn't understand all the complexities of the message. As if the two short sentences were simply too much to comprehend.

But really, I was just stalling.

It was an effort to sort out my emotions, which were primarily dominated by fear. The fear and a fair amount of excitement hit me at once. Fear of the Germans. Fear of my father. Fear of the unknown. And on a certain level, fear of Dominic. Of seeing him again.

I was scared that Dominic might tell me he didn't want to have anything to do with me anymore, that I was too much for him, had too much of a temper. Of course, he probably would have just said that in the letter.

But I was excited, too. Other than our time together in the mountains, we had fallen in love through our letters, and I knew things might be different in person, as things are sometimes easier to say in writing compared to face-to-face.

He was taking a risk trying to see me in person. More of a risk in fact than walking up and down the mountain. If he were caught here, the penalty would be severe and immediate. And if we were discovered together, the penalty for him would be much greater than for me. He would be sent immediately to the front, and from the sounds of the fighting, he would not last long. On the other hand, I wasn't certain what would happen to me. Certainly a stern reprimand from Zizi Checcone and a tired look of disappointment from Colonel Wolff. Of course, my punishment could turn out to be much more severe.

The Varano barn: a sagging, dilapidated structure pushed all the way back to the forest's edge at the base of the mountain. It was the perfect place for Dominic; he could come down the mountain at night, slip from the forest into the back of the barn unnoticed. And at the first sign of trouble, he could be back in the safety of the woods in seconds. It was a good choice.

Was it a good choice for me to go to see him, though? To be with him in secret? This was much more than just hiding love letters beneath a rock. This was a big step.

I had never been in love before, had never agreed to meet secretly with any boy, much less a boy of whom I knew my father did not approve.

My feet remained rooted to the ground. My knees bent, as if to step forward, but my feet were not yet ready to cooperate. A hundred possibilities of what would happen went through my mind, all of them bad. What can I say? That's the way my mind worked. Imagine the worst.

With monumental effort, I turned myself around, and faced the direction in which the Varano barn lay. I glanced to the left—that was the way home. I made my decision, and walked confidently in the direction of the Varano barn.

I walked quickly, checking frequently to make sure I wasn't being followed. My imagination ran wild; everywhere there were Germans, or, nearly as bad, old women from the village who would see and tell my father that his daughter was secretly meeting a boy of whom he did not approve. I'm not sure whom I would rather have been caught by.

Within minutes, the barn came into sight. It was even more run-down than I remembered; it had been some time since I'd seen it. Its rafters were sagging, the door sat crookedly on its hinges, and the window frames were stripped of any paint. The barn was mostly stone, and it seemed to be cracking everywhere.

I walked briskly past it, down a steep grade, then cut across a shallow field to the edge of the woods. From behind a tree, I watched for any movement in or around the barn. I saw nothing. Something rustled in the undergrowth behind me, but it faded away slowly. Probably a squirrel.

Scanning the area around the barn and the houses farther away, I saw no movement, no sign that anyone had followed me. But it was getting close to dark now, and I had no way of knowing for sure. This was a gamble, in every sense. Although I felt melodramatic in thinking it, there was no getting around the fact that what I was doing now would most likely change my life forever.

Mustering up as much courage as possible, I made my way slowly along the tree line, keeping the barn on the periphery of my vision, while I kept my eyes scanning the surrounding homes and fields. Again, nothing seemed out of the ordinary, and I breathed a sigh of relief when I reached the back of the barn. I looked at the crumbling back wall, covered with vines and smelling of decaying timber.

There was no sign of Dominic.

Wishing not to use the enormous front doors, I moved along the side until I found a half door, probably used for livestock. I ducked underneath and was inside. The musty smell of old hay washed over me, not entirely unpleasant. In fact, with the cold rain coming down harder every minute outside, the barn was cozy in a way.

"Dominic?" I whispered softly, scanning the darkness. Slowly I began to make my way around, feeling with each foot before setting it down. I stepped on something soft and squishy; chills went down my spine. A soft squeaking sound called from a corner. Field mice, most likely.

Suddenly, a hand clamped across my mouth.

CHAPTER THIRTY-EIGHT

—

Shhh."
I felt a hand turn me around and then from out of the darkness I saw the faint glow of Dominic Giancarlo's beautiful blue eyes.

"You made enough noise," he murmured, laughing softly and moving his hand from my mouth to the side of my neck. "Good thing you aren't a spy; we would all be doomed."

"Very funny. Nice place to pick. So romantic."

He still hadn't taken his hands off me.

"What, do you want me to meet you in the town square?" he said. "In case you haven't noticed, there's a war going on."

"Why don't you—?"

He kissed me then, hard. His lips didn't move on mine, but he pressed hard. I threw my arms around his broad shoulders, and his arms circled my waist like big snakes. We broke apart, smiled at each other, then kissed again.

"The letters . . ." he started to say, but I pressed a finger to his lips.

"I know," I said. Then I kissed him again.

He put his hands on my shoulders and gently pushed me back.

"No, I have to tell you something."

I rolled my eyes, then folded my arms across my chest.

"This better be good."

"I used parts of the letters from Luigi Iacobelli's book."

"I know."

"But only because the letters said what I was feeling, and said it better than I could have."

"What, are you going to have this book with you for the rest of your life? When you are feeling an emotion, look up the right chapter and then tell me about it?"

"No, I'm telling you that's why I did it," he said. "And I know it was the easy thing to do. From now on, they will be my own words."

"You are honest, Dominic; that's one of the reasons I love you. Your honesty is more beautiful than any words you could copy out of a book. You know that?"

He hugged me tightly.

"And you are more beautiful than anything in the world," he said.

We kissed again and he lifted me, carried me across the barn to a mound of old hay bales. He set me down and lay next to me, one arm under me, the other caressing my body.

His hair felt soft beneath my hands, his lips gentle and firm. I felt a warmth in my loins I had never felt before, and my body surged with emotions. His breath became ragged and he broke away from me to catch his breath.

Thoughts of my father came into my head, thoughts of Zizi Checcone, and the German soldiers close by. But I pushed them from my mind. *Just awhile longer,* I thought. *Just awhile longer and then I will go back to that existence soon enough.*

"I have dreamed of this moment since you left," he said, turning to smile at me. I was looking up into the darkness of the barn's rafters.

"I've thought about it, too. I just thought it wouldn't happen until after the Germans left. I guess I didn't realize how foolish you are."

"Love does that," he said.

I closed my eyes and luxuriated in the warmth, the heat of my body; I could still feel his hands on me; his eagerness and desire consumed me, made me feel alive. Until then, I had always felt like a girl, but now, with the smell of hay beneath me, and the scent of Dominic on my cheeks, I felt, for the first time in my life, like a woman.

I leaned over to whisper that into his ear and it was then that I felt the chill of cold steel against my throat.

My eyes opened and I saw Schlemmer kneeling above me. A knife was in his hand, pressed against my neck, and in his other hand was a pistol, pointed squarely at Dominic, who still had his eyes closed.

Schlemmer spoke in broken Italian.

"Ah, you play the saint with me, the whore with him."

Dominic's eyes snapped open and he started to rise, but Schlemmer's pistol forced him back down.

I was going to die in this barn. I had allowed myself a dream, a brief one, and now it was going to be cut apart by an evil German. I thought of my father, first losing his wife, and now his eldest daughter. It was too much.

"Turn over, hands behind your head," Schlemmer said to Dominic, gesturing with the pistol. Dominic complied.

Schlemmer's voice was thick with disgust and loathing. "Coward," he said. "Hide in the mountain from the fighting, but come down to be with your whore, hiding in a barn. There is no such thing as an Italian man. There are Italian women and Italian cowards."

His breath reeked, a sour smell that renewed its strength with each breath he took.

"You disgust me," Schlemmer said. "We should kill all of you, forget about the Americans. At least they fight."

Schlemmer turned to me and, with his pistol still on Dominic, slowly trailed the tip of his knife down my neck to my chest. His blade went between my breasts and I inhaled sharply. Dominic turned his head slightly and Schlemmer trained his pistol at his eye, grinning luridly at him. "Yes," he said. "Do something, Italian hero."

When Dominic looked away, Schlemmer turned back to me. The point of his knife hooked on my dress and he lifted quickly, slicing the material. He reinserted his knife and slowly pulled down, tearing my dress and undergarments open and exposing my breasts. I instinctively brought my hands up to cover them, but he jerked the knife quickly, saying, "Ah-ah-ah," and I stopped my hands in midair, then dropped them back to my side.

As his eyes devoured my body, he started to talk.

"So there I am, sitting on a chair outside the hospital, unable to sleep from the medicines the doctors are giving me for my shrapnel wounds, when what do I see but a beautiful young Italian girl sneaking toward a barn."

The knife moved down over my stomach, the material being cut in half.

"I decide to follow. I can't sleep anyway, right? So I see her go into this barn. I wait. I look for a door where I can slip in quietly and watch the action and oh, what action I see!" He laughed in the darkness and I could smell his foul breath, visualize his stained teeth.

"I see you two rolling around and I think to myself, if anyone's going to fuck this girl, it's going to be me," Schlemmer said.

His knifepoint reached my pubic hair and he stopped, then pulled slightly so my dress would reveal more. His breathing was increasing and his hand was starting to shake. The knife went down farther. My body shook and I started to cry.

He raised the knife back up to my chest and pulled my dress wider, so that my breasts were completely exposed.

"Ah, so beautiful, so beautiful."

He bent down and placed his mouth around my nipple and as he did so, Dominic lashed out with his hand and struck the gun toward the rafters. The gun exploded and then Dominic was launching himself over me atop Schlemmer and the two of them rolled away, struggling madly for control of both weapons. I scrabbled away on my back and could think of nothing to do but watch in horror as they grunted and thrashed in the hay.

After what seemed an impossibly long time, Dominic drove his knee with immense force into Schlemmer's side and sent him flying several feet from him. Something black and gleaming spun away from them into the dark along the wall as Schlemmer flew, and when the gun landed, both of them looked wildly after it.

Schlemmer looked away from the lost prize too late. Dominic was already on his feet and swinging from the hip, a sweeping blow packed with power that connected flush on Schlemmer's jaw with the sound of a two-by-four cracking a pig's skull. But Schlemmer was jabbing with his knife. Just as the punch landed, the blade sank into Dominic's side. Schlemmer went down from the blow and Dominic jumped back; his left hand went to his right side and came away bloody.

Schlemmer, stunned, regained his footing, but Dominic lunged forward, head-butting the German and driving them both back into the hay again.

Dominic held on to Schlemmer's wrist and tried to break his grip on the knife. They twisted and writhed, battling for control of it, until Dominic cracked Schlemmer's hand against a wood post and the knife sailed over both of their heads. They broke, rolled in opposite directions, and then crashed at each other, but Dominic was faster and landed a sharp uppercut that snapped Schlemmer's head back.

Suddenly, the fog cleared in my head and I made a beeline for the gun, scrambling across the floor like a crab.

I was about five feet from the wall where it had landed when Dominic punched Schlemmer in the stomach and he fell back, landing between the gun and me.

The German jumped to his feet and rushed Dominic, ramming him in the stomach, and they crashed again to the ground with Schlemmer on top. He brought his fists back and crashed them with ferocious power into Dominic's face. I started crawling toward the wall again and actually spied the gun, but Schlemmer saw me, jumped off Dominic, and lunged after me, getting hold of my ankle. He pulled me toward him as he rose to his knees.

He was laughing, a look of insanity on his face.

He heaved me to one side, diving for the gun. Suddenly, a shadow passed over me and Dominic landed on top of the German. A flash of steel, and then Dominic sank the knife deep into Schlemmer's throat.

The German had his hand around the gun, but Dominic clamped down on it with his own hand, and pulled the knife in one long, cutting motion across Schlemmer's neck. Dominic repositioned himself and pinned Schlemmer's head to the ground. A fountain of blood gurgled from the German's neck as he bled to death. Soon, the flow of blood went down to a trickle, then it seemed to stop altogether.

All movement stopped, and the barn was silent.

After several minutes, Dominic rolled off Schlemmer, stood, and turned the German over. I stood, shaking, and stepped forward.

Schlemmer's lifeless eyes stared at the barn's ceiling, a long gash making a second obscene smile along his neck. His head was nearly cut off, hanging on by a thin strip of tissue.

Dominic turned and retched, wincing and clutching his side as he did so.

He was still bleeding.

I made him sit down, then took off his shirt. The wound was nasty, but not deep. Apparently it had gone in, then caromed off, cutting much flesh, but not reaching deeply enough to hit any vital organs.

I forced Dominic's hand open and took the knife from him, then cut one of his sleeves off. I tied it around him, pressing the widest part of the material into his wound.

"You have to go back up the mountain. You have no choice."

He nodded, keeping his eyes averted.

I looked down and saw my exposed breasts. I took the loose ends of my dress and tried to hook them together, then tied them in a small knot. It would have to do. It was fully dark outside and I could get home unnoticed. I would have to destroy the dress so Zizi Checcone couldn't see it.

Both of our eyes fell on Schlemmer.

"We have to hide him," Dominic said.

I looked around the barn. It was empty save for the rotten hay bales and some old planks of wood. A broken plow, too heavy to move, was in a corner.

"The hay bales. We have to hide him underneath," I said.

We moved them with great effort, then dragged Schlemmer—I had his boot heels; Dominic grasped him underneath the arms. We did not take his gun, as discovery by the Germans would mean instant execution.

We pushed a bale off the top of the stack and it landed on Schlemmer. Then we arranged the other bales around him and quickly covered over the blood spots with loose hay.

"They will miss him," Dominic said.

"Maybe they'll think he ran away. The colonel said he was a disturbed boy."

"I think he was right."

"We just have to pray that no one finds him," I said. "The Americans are advancing, maybe . . ."

"Maybe, maybe, maybe . . ." Dominic spat out angrily. "You will be in danger."

"If I get home unnoticed, no one will think I killed him. A little girl killing a big, tough German soldier? Never!"

We both looked outside.

"We both must go. Now," I said.

Dominic looked at me, his eyes filling with tears.

We kissed and left the barn together, our hands clasped.

"Don't worry, Dom. We will see each other again. God will watch over us."

We hugged and kissed one final time, then Dominic disappeared unsteadily into the woods. I prayed that he would make it up the mountain, a long walk hard enough without a knife wound oozing blood.

I made my way home, walking. I passed the houses where people were getting their last, precious moments of sleep and I broke into a run, my feet flying, my legs pumping so that I felt like I was soaring over the ground, suspended in the air by an invisible mixture of fear and horror and, strangely enough, love.

CHAPTER THIRTY-NINE

—

For a week, nothing happened. I received no note from Dominic, but that meant nothing. Even if he made it back to the hideout in the mountains, he would not come back down again. He would need to rest and let his wound heal. And if he didn't make it, I shuddered at the thought there would be no more notes, ever.

Although I had suffered no physical wound, the week was one of recovery for me, too. The shock of Schlemmer's attack and the ensuing fight still clung to me; every time I heard the sound of a German I pictured Schlemmer appearing in the doorway, his head lolling crookedly to one side, blood seeping from his throat.

But as the days passed, I calmed down and felt that maybe Dominic and I would be lucky; maybe no one would miss Schlemmer, and even if they did, maybe no one would think to look inside an abandoned barn beneath some bales of hay.

Exactly one week later, when black clouds rolled in and light rain began to weigh down the dust of Casalvieri, a German soldier on crutches came to the house, followed by Becher, and it was then that I knew for certain my luck had run out.

They came inside the house, and Becher beckoned to me. The man on crutches looked me up and down, said something to Becher, who turned and looked at me again, then responded, also in German, to the wounded man. He shifted on his crutches and looked at me, then a flicker of recognition passed over his eyes.

My blood ran cold.

The man on crutches nodded again and said something to Becher that was clearly in the affirmative.

Becher turned to me, his cold blue eyes flat and lifeless. He said something to the man on crutches, who turned and left the house. I could hear the sound of pushing and grunting as he swung himself along.

Pulling up a chair, Becher sat and looked at me as I stood before him.

"So how did a little girl like you manage to kill one of my soldiers?" There was a smile on his face, but no humor behind it.

When I answered, my voice was even.

"I've killed no one. That's your job."

He laughed out loud.

"Yes, and since you, or whoever, killed one of my soldiers, I will have many more to exterminate." He emphasized the last word, as if we Italians were rodents.

I said nothing as he continued to watch me.

"So you know nothing about Schlemmer's death? Even though the soldier who was just here said he was sitting with Schlemmer outside the hospital a week ago when they saw you walk by?" Becher said. "It was very late at night; these soldiers, with all of their medications, they have trouble getting to sleep sometimes."

He seemed to be almost compassionate when he spoke of his soldiers.

"He said you were walking quickly. Schlemmer apparently decided to follow you. And no one has seen him alive since."

"I go for walks at night," I said, and shrugged. "Ask anyone. Ask Colonel Wolff."

"I think we'll leave Colonel Wolff out of this matter."

"I never saw Schlemmer," I said. "If he came after me, he never caught up. I walk pretty fast and if he was at the hospital he must have been hurt; maybe he couldn't keep up the pace."

He laughed out loud at that.

"You are a good liar, aren't you?" Becher said. "Well, of course you are—you're an Italian." He smiled. "I admire you. You are a brave girl; no one ever doubted that."

I shrugged again.

Suddenly, he brightened, as if struck by a thought. "Perhaps you would like to see how we can make you talk, make you tell the truth? I know some men who would love to get their hands on a beautiful young girl like you. I would let them do the same things to you that they did to that other girl, what was her name?" He looked at the ceiling as if he were trying to remember. "Lauretta!" He snapped his fingers. "Yes, Lauretta. Now, you two were good friends, weren't you?"

I ignored him, and the anger that rose within me at the mention of Lauretta's name.

"I would tell them the same thing," I said. "I don't know what happened to the soldier named Schlemmer."

He sighed heavily, but then one of the men from the jeep outside called to him as their portable radio burst with German shouting. Becher stepped to the door and called out to another soldier who was waiting outside; he was young, blond, and had his rifle slung over his shoulder. Becher gestured toward me.

"Keep your eye on her until I return. Do not let her leave the house or your sight."

The soldier nodded and stepped inside the doorway to let Becher pass, but Becher stopped and turned back to me.

"I will be back shortly. Don't go anywhere. This matter is not yet settled." He looked me in the eye, but I returned his look with a blank stare. Then he walked briskly to a waiting truck that quickly started up and roared away.

I went to the hearth and stirred the fire. The house was silent; Zizi Checcone, Emidio, and Iole were doing the wash in the natural springs east of Casalvieri. They would be back soon.

My mind raced and I forced myself to concentrate on the facts. For one, I knew the Germans had no way of knowing what had happened to Schlemmer. If they had found any evidence linking me directly to his death, I most likely would have been executed on the spot. The fact that Becher asked me for information meant that Dominic had gotten away. I thanked God for that.

I also knew that Wolff had told Papa that if one German soldier died, ten villagers would be executed. That's what Becher meant when he said more people would die; he believed Schlemmer's death would be avenged. But would Wolff approve of that?

There were too many questions and not enough answers. Suddenly, fear washed over me and my hands started shaking. I wanted Papa here to protect me, I wanted to run to my mother, I wanted to be far away from anyone who could hurt me. And then the realization flooded me like ice-cold water, that I might die today. Becher might have me stand against a wall and have his men fire their rifles at me. Or worse, he would have some of them take me behind the house and rape me.

I stayed like that for a long time, I'm not sure how long, but I heard the sound of voices, children's voices, and I got to my feet. The German soldier was standing where Becher had left him, watching me dispassionately, not a trace of sympathy or even curiosity.

The door opened and Iole bounded in with Emidio right on her heels. I looked out the door and saw Zizi Checcone coming toward the house, a heavy basket of laundry on her shoulder. She was looking away from the house, to the right. My eyes followed hers, and I saw a long line of German vehicles coming down the mountain and into town.

Colonel Wolff was in the lead vehicle.

I motioned for Zizi Checcone to come inside quickly. I needed to get them in and out of the house before Wolff arrived. If there was going to be any retaliation for Schlemmer's murder, I wanted it to be directed toward me alone and I wanted the three of them to be as far away as possible.

Zizi Checcone was ten yards away from the house, her short legs carrying her as fast as they could manage, when a deep rumble shook the ground and I looked toward the western side of the mountain.

Zizi Checcone stopped and stood still, looking in the same direction.

As the long line of German vehicles drew toward the house, the entire western side of the mountain erupted in a tremendous explosion: A mixture of fire and black smoke, dirt, and debris rained down upon Casalvieri, turning day into night.

CHAPTER FORTY

—

G o! Go! Go!" Wolff yelled to his driver. A German soldier who had followed the armored convoy on foot ran to Wolff's car and piled onto the back.

The Germans were leaving Casalvieri. The Allies were bombing their retreat, trying to kill as many of them as possible, probably for revenge after the bloody battle of Mt. Cassino.

Wolff barked a command at the driver of the second vehicle: a large two-track carrying at least twenty men. The driver of the two-track followed Wolff's car as it came to a stop in front of the house. Wolff heaved himself out of the truck as a man began directing the rest of the vehicles to follow. Men raced into the house and then back out, carrying the few meager belongings that were still in their possession. I watched as one truck went to the Ingrelli household, where soldiers who were able to walk or run clambered aboard the waiting truck. The ones who couldn't travel would be left behind, prisoners of war at the mercy of the Allies.

As men raced to and from, carrying rifles and packs, I saw Becher emerge from a car.

Colonel Wolff entered the house.

"Benedetta!" His eyes fell on me.

Iole and Emidio were huddled around my legs, hugging them, and Zizi Checcone was standing near the hearth with the laundry at her feet, uncertain what to do. I pushed the children toward Zizi Checcone as Wolff reached for me. There simply hadn't been enough time to get them out of the house, especially with Wolff approaching the house's only exit.

He put his arms around me and I flinched, half expecting to feel the cold metal of a gun barrel pressed against my head. This was the moment we had both longed for and dreaded; the Germans were leaving, and the question was, what would they leave behind?

Colonel Wolff grabbed me and hugged me tightly. His medals pressed against me and poked my chest; the rough stubble of his unshaven face scraped my cheeks.

"Benedetta," he said. "You must tell me what happened between you and Schlemmer. I want the truth."

Becher appeared in the doorway and we both turned. Wolff looked back at me.

"I saw him following me and I ran," I said. "I cut through a barn then circled around and went in the other direction. I never saw him again. I figured that I had tricked him."

"She's lying," Becher said.

"I believe you," Wolff said to me. He turned to Becher. "She is not lying. She has taken care of me and my men, and now this matter is of no importance. We must hurry."

"No importance?" Becher asked, his face reddening. "Since when is the death of one of your men not important? Since when is there not enough time to avenge the murder of a German soldier?"

"Since the Americans will be coming over that mountain any minute now, and the longer you delay us creates more time for the

Allies to kill our soldiers!" Wolff was shouting. "If you really care about our men, you will forget this and go!"

"His death must be avenged!" Becher shouted. "These people must understand that Germans are their superiors!"

"Are you insane? We are losing the war! We are losing this country! Our leader has stretched us too thin, spent too much time murdering Jews!" Wolff moved toward Becher, his hands clenched in fists. "Look at you! Look at your arrogant German pride! This is what has been the death of us!"

Becher took a step back and for a moment I thought he was going to run outside and climb into a car. But he did not.

Instead, he coolly removed his pistol from the leather holster on his hip and faced Wolff.

"You are a traitor," he said quietly.

And then he shot Wolff between the eyes.

Wolff fell back toward me; his heavy body crashed to the floor. His head landed at my feet. The soft gray hair, now coming apart in bloody chunks, was splattered on my shoes.

"The penalty for treason is death!" Becher yelled at the dead man on the floor. "Traitor!" he said, and spat on Wolff.

The room reeked of gunpowder. Iole and Emidio were sobbing loudly against Zizi Checcone's legs. The old woman watched, frozen.

"You," he barked at Zizi Checcone. "Take those two and go stand against the barn! Now!"

Iole and Emidio were in tears as Zizi Checcone herded them out the door.

Becher crossed the room and stood before me. "See what you have done?" he said, then slapped me across the face. The blow knocked me to the ground and I tasted blood in my mouth.

I staggered to my feet and watched as Becher removed Wolff's belt with the pistol still in the holster. His face was a mask of stone, unmoving; his eyes seemed to be frozen straight ahead, as if they were locked on a target.

"Gather all the food you have and bring it outside to me!" Becher said. "Then stand with the others against the barn! Now! Move!"

He walked out toward his car. In the distance, I saw Zizi Checcone standing with Iole and Emidio against the wall. They were watching the house. Zizi Checcone was crossing herself.

I rushed to the kitchen and grabbed the last loaf of bread and a big hunk of cheese. It was all we had left. A small burlap sack holding two small onions sat on the floor against the hearth. I emptied the bag of the onions, placed the cheese inside, then opened the small cupboard in the corner of the kitchen and grabbed the hand grenade Emidio had brought home. It again felt incredibly heavy in my hands for its size and I hesitated for a split second, truly thought about what I was going to do. And then I moved.

I turned over the loaf of bread and gouged out a small hole, then tucked the hand grenade inside, lodging it in sideways with the grenade's pin sticking out. I looped one finger through the grenade's pin, then gathered cloth with my remaining fingers so that I could lift the bag.

I stood and ran outside toward Becher. He was walking back toward the house to find me when I emerged, running hard for him. Five feet from him, I pulled my finger from the inside of the bread and the hand grenade's pin came with it. I let the ring slip from my finger and I grabbed the bag with my other hand.

I gave the bag to Becher, then turned and ran toward Zizi Checcone.

As I ran, I looked over my shoulder. Becher was five feet from his car. He stepped toward the vehicle and I saw it all happen so slowly. One step. Two steps. His head was raised, looking toward the top of the mountain from which the front edge of American tanks could be seen.

I heard nothing but silence. My feet pounded the ground; there was no air in my lungs. My head spun.

A third step. He was now next to the car, extending his arms to place the bag of bread and cheese on the front passenger seat next to Colonel Wolff's pistol belt.

I turned and looked to Emidio and Iole. My eyes locked on to theirs. Their mouths were open as I ran.

A flash erupted from the mountain as a German artillery round pounded at the Americans' advance.

And then I was flying. The ground briefly moved away from me as I felt my feet fly up and my body rotated. Was I dead? Maybe I was flying to Heaven to see my mother, to be with her. Maybe at last someone would protect me. But then, I reasoned, I would already be dead and why would I need someone to protect me?

That was my last thought as the ground flew up at me, and I hit hard, the shock crushing my chest. I felt something trickle from my ears.

I rolled over and over and over. Brief flashes of a car on fire, of Zizi Checcone and Emidio and Iole on the ground, a sound deep and powerful washed over me, followed by darkness.

CHAPTER FORTY-ONE

—

A h, the angel awakens."
I tried to open my eyes but the brightness blinded me, and a horrible pain shot through my forehead, feeling a hundred times worse than any headache I'd ever had. My eyes watered and I cracked my eyes to slits, just enough to see a rounded pear shape, blurred through my tears, standing at the foot of my bed.

"Papa?"

"Shhh, relax, Benedetta," my father said. "Don't try to move; you've been through—"

I swung my feet off the bed and tried to rise, but the pain wracked my head again and I felt faint as I drifted, preparing myself for a collision with the cold floor. But Papa's hands went beneath my arms and he hugged me to him, his rough shirt scratching me through my pajama top. He laid me back on the bed and covered me with a blanket.

"Sleep, Benedetta. You are still not well. When you wake up, you'll have some soup."

"The *Germanesí* . . ."

"They are gone. The Americans are here," he said. And then, as an afterthought, he added, "I am here, too."

"Iole, Emidio . . ."

"They are fighting with each other as usual."

"Zizi Checcone."

"Downstairs cooking."

I hesitated, wanted to ask but wasn't sure how much my father knew and how he would feel. He read my mind.

"Dominic is here too."

I felt a flood of relief.

"Is he . . . ?"

"He's all right. The wound became infected, but the Americans gave him some medicine and it's better. When you've rested some more, you can see him."

I pulled the blanket up tighter, holding it underneath my chin.

My father stood, watching me, and just as I was falling asleep I either heard, or dreamed, that he leaned down and whispered in my ear.

"I love you."

With my eyes closed, I concentrated on relaxing my body, muscle by muscle, nerve by nerve. I started with my feet and then worked my way up, until I was able to finally relax my face, my clenched jaw.

The Germans were gone.

Sleep came to me quickly then, and I dreamed of the night the Germans first arrived. Of the morning when I came down the stairs to see Colonel Wolff and my father at the kitchen table. In the dream, Colonel Wolff saw his own body on the floor, just like it was after Becher shot him. And in the dream, Wolff asked my father what he was doing with a dead German officer in his house.

I woke before my father answered.

The ceiling of the bedroom looked the same to me. Its thin cracks were reassuring to me; they even looked beautiful. Maybe because I realized they were ours again. This house was ours. Our lives were ours.

It was all over now.

And I was alive.

I crossed myself and thanked God again for blessing me.

CHAPTER FORTY-TWO

—

The flames crackled and sizzled as juice from the pig dripped and splattered onto the thick logs of the bonfire. The people of Casalvieri, as well as a few American and British soldiers, were assembled in the village square.

American flour had been turned into hundreds of loaves of thick, delicious bread. Barrels of wine, hidden in cellars throughout the occupation, had been brought out, along with the pig. The pig that had never seen the light of day, that had wandered around in a daze upon being freed, then diagnosed as irreparably damaged by confinement, was being roasted in celebration of the village's new-found freedom.

I had yet to see Dominic; I knew he would go to his home in Roselli to check on his mother and his brothers, then he would come for me. My palms were sweaty and I paced around the crowd, not relaxed, keeping my mind occupied with the job of exchanging hugs and kisses, caught up in the excitement of a second chance.

My father stood in the center of the crowd, in charge of roasting the pig and saying a few words. He raised his glass of wine and toasted the people of Casalvieri, as well as the Allied soldiers. There was a hearty cheer in response to his words and then people fell to drinking.

Though I would not be eating the pig, nor would Iole and Emidio—I had seen why the pig was fat—it somehow seemed appropriate that the people who had taken so much from Casalvieri, who had caused so much starvation, were now feeding those same people.

"Benedetta."

I turned and there was Dominic. He looked taller, thinner than I remembered him, his eyes blue and teeth white. He smiled at me. My goodness, he was handsome.

He rushed to me and I threw my arms around him. We hugged and hugged until he winced, and then I pulled back.

"I'm sorry!" I said.

"It's all right. It is healing."

He put his hands on my shoulders and looked at me seriously.

"How are you? I heard what you did," he said. "You know you are a hero?"

"Have some more wine. You're not talking any sense, anyway."

He smiled, a tired smile, an old smile on a face too young to be wearing it. He took me in his arms again, and we stood there for many minutes, long enough to have a small crowd gather around us, singing.

We moved toward the small fountain that stood at the center of town and sat on its edge. Dominic told me about his hike up the mountain, about how he passed out several times, only to get up and put one foot in front of the other until he collapsed at the cabin and the men brought him inside, made a bandage, and slowly nursed him back to health.

"Did you tell them the truth?"

He shook his head.

"Only your father."

I waited.

"I think he wanted to kill me. But he helped me get better, took me for walks, made broth to help me get my strength back, and cleaned my wound to prevent infection," he said. "I figured if he wanted to kill me, he wasn't doing a very good job."

I saw Papa going through the crowd, talking, shaking hands, toasting. God had truly blessed me with him.

When Dominic was done filling in the details of his recovery, I told him about Becher and Wolff, and the hand grenade. I was surprised at how much the retelling affected me. Even after telling Papa and others, it was still hard for me to get through. When I was in my room resting, I heard someone downstairs talking about Becher being blown to bits. They found one of his legs on the roof of the house.

Now, I finished telling Dominic the story and he shook his head.

"You are amazing, Benedetta. No wonder I love you so much."

I blushed at the word, and then blushed more when my father approached.

"Just the two people I want to talk to," he said.

CHAPTER FORTY-THREE

—

A merica?" I asked, incredulously.
My father nodded. "America."

The celebration was winding down; most of the people had gone home to begin their lives again. Someone had passed out small cups of coffee to the remaining celebrants.

"But why?" My heart was pounding and my head started to hurt again. "Things are finally back to normal," I reasoned. "The Germans are gone. We can plant new crops. Rebuild. Why do you want to leave?"

"Zi Antonio," my father said.

"Zi Antonio? Your little brother?" I asked. "What does he have to do with this?"

"He is in America. He started his own construction company before the war, remember? Well, before the Germans came here, he wrote me and said he needed a partner, but I told him no."

"You told him no," I said.

"But now he sent a letter and said that when the war is over, the American soldiers will come home and start families and build lots and lots of houses," my father said. "He says life is better there. More food. Jobs. Medicine. It is a better place to raise children."

I thought about the crops, about the damage to the village, and then the stories of America. About the wealth. About big houses and jobs that pay lots of money.

Reading my mind, my father said, "And look at what we have left. Our crops are ruined; we will be starving for at least two more years. And then what?"

I could think of nothing else to say. Except one thing. What about Dominic?

Again, my father knew what I was thinking.

"That's why I didn't want you two to fall in love," Papa said.

Dominic looked at his feet.

"Too late," I said.

Now it was Dominic's turn to blush. My father watched him slowly turn red, then spoke.

"Dominic, I have nothing against you. I think you are a fine young man, and I know that you would treat my daughter with respect."

He clamped his hand over Dominic's.

"But I do not want to leave anyone behind." His eyes clouded over and I knew he was thinking about my mother. "Benedetta is coming with us to America and I will not hear of anything else."

"When?" I asked.

My father shrugged. "When the war is over everywhere. And the Americans go back to their country. Then we will go."

My father turned to Dominic. "If you can make it to America," he said, "I would be honored for you to call on Benedetta."

Dominic looked at me. His eyes were watering. "Yes, I will."

My father left us then.

"You will come to America, Dominic?" I asked.

"I will come to America, Benedetta."

"Do you swear you will?"

"I swear to God I will."

I hugged Dominic, clinging to him. I whispered in his ear that if he didn't keep his promise I would come back and bring him to America myself.

"Enough of this serious talk," my father called to us. "Let's get drunk."

CHAPTER FORTY-FOUR

—

We passed through the fog on our way down the mountain. The old bus alternately chugged and braked, smoking and squeaking until the orange glow of Naples came into view, the sunlight sparkling on the Mediterranean just beyond.

It was the first time I had ever been to Naples, but there would be no wandering through the shops and restaurants of the biggest city I had ever been to. The bus would take us directly to the harbor where a ship sat docked, waiting to take us to the Land of Opportunity.

The good-byes in Casalvieri took nearly a week to complete. We were invited to dinners put together by groups of families; my father at one time or another had helped everyone in Casalvieri, and it was important to pay our respects to everyone, lest we insult a single person.

It had been almost a year since the Germans left. The war was over now, Japan had surrendered, and the Americans were returning to their country, ready to start families and build houses. Lots and lots of houses.

Our land and home were sold. We were officially a family without a country until we landed in America and found a place to live, a place to call our own.

I had said my good-byes to Dominic. The bond between the two of us was eternal; I knew that deep in my heart. His vows of love and mine were genuine; our fates were sealed together now, even if our physical selves were divided by an ocean.

Dominic would stay with his three brothers and mother to help them plant the new crops and get things in order, then he would come with his younger brother to America. If they did well, they would send for the mother and brother.

The bus took us directly to the harbor where the huge ship, called the *Volcania*, waited patiently.

A man offered to take our luggage, but we refused, finding a seat on the deck and tucking the small trunks beneath our legs. Our valuables and the money from the sale of the house and land were neatly sewn into a leather satchel that circled my father's waist.

It would remain there until we reached Zi Antonio's.

Zizi Checcone, dressed in a flowery print dress instead of her usual black, her hair pulled back neatly behind her head, sat next to my father. It had come as no surprise when Papa told me they were going to get married before leaving for America. I had known they were falling in love. I thought about my mother and I knew she would be happy for Papa.

Their wedding had been a village celebration, a chance to reaffirm life and a new beginning for them, as well as for Casalvieri.

The last of the passengers boarded the ship, and the sailors cast off the huge ropes holding us to shore. We pushed out into the harbor with a thunderous blast from the ship's horn and applause from the hundreds of people who had come to see off their loved ones.

I looked behind me, where Papa and Zizi Checcone sat next to one another, Iole and Emidio on their laps, wide-eyed and excited. They were smiling at me. The strong breeze pulled back Iole's long hair and she raised her hands out as if she were going to fly. Emidio hugged Zizi Checcone harder, his face buried in her bosom.

Thick black smoke billowed from the ship's stacks, and we seemed to merely creep out of the harbor, despite the mighty rumbling of the engines beneath our feet. I leaned over the side, my fingers gripping the white metal railing as I looked into the water below, trying to get a feel for the actual speed of the ship.

The water was dark—black, really—and it caressed the rusty hull of the ship, tiny bubbles of froth fizzing before being swept under thick waves.

I heard the sound of the water, felt the wind on my face, and watched as the dark waters swirled behind us, their peaks and troughs briefly marking our passage before reshaping into the flat calm that erased history with silent ease.

ACKNOWLEDGMENTS

——

I would like to thank the wonderful people at Lake Union and Amazon Publishing, in particular Jodi Warshaw, for bringing this story to life. Additional thanks go to the Giancarlo and Carlesimo families. And finally, endless gratitude to Rocco and Rosa Giancarlo for sharing your stories, your lives, and your love.

ABOUT THE AUTHOR

—

Dani Amore is a novelist living in Los Angeles, California. You can learn more about her at http://www.daniamore.com.